FOR HER PROTECTION

For Her Protection

Dria Andersen

Copyright

Dedication

To my husband, who was my sounding board, my cheerleader, my critique partner, and all the things I needed to finish this project. I appreciate every hour, every word of input, and most of all, your unwavering support.

To my family, who had to deal with mommy being on in another world for hours at a time. Thank you for your patience.

To my sister Tina, who reads everything I write and gives me honest feedback and encouragement, thank you mucho mucho. I appreciate your continued support and cheerleading! To my aunt Cathy who gave me my first love of romance stories, I thank you for allowing me to raid your bookshelf.

Thank you to every fan who continues to stick with me while telling the stories playing in my head. I appreciate each and every one of you. Also, I would like to give a special thanks to Pikko House for the feedback and help I get from your alpha readers.

Contents

One

The crush of the crowd was instantly familiar. Strangely, it was one of the things Julissa missed about Motsi gatherings. Animal shifters of all types gathered in the ballroom, dressed in the various hues of red, celebrating...what in the world were they celebrating now? She shook her head and took another sip of champagne. She honestly didn't know, and frankly, most of those in attendance probably didn't care. Any reason to gather, gossip and show-off. It was one of the perks of being a part of high shifter society.

Her father was on the Tri-council, and her family was one of the founding members of the Motsi society. Micah's position afforded Julissa many privileges that she'd enjoyed over the years. The lavish parties, the safety and protection the insular community granted had all been at her fingertips.

The tri-council, or ruling three as they were called, was responsible for controlling and governing the shifters of Eastfield. The city was divided into three parts, the cats on the Southside, bears on the North, and wolf shifters on the Eastside. The West side was neutral and home to humans and some shifters who kept themselves separate from the Motsi, though they still answered to the council. Her father had been in his job since she was born, holding on to that position with a firm hand that meant strength for some, and fear for others.

Julissa was happy to be home. For a year after law school, it had been touch and go. She'd traveled for that year, appeasing her mother under the guise of figuring out what she wanted to do with her life. But she already knew. It took her months of begging her father and Silas Knight's assistant to get her an interview with him. Finally, after a year, she'd gotten the job she most wanted. Silas Knight was liaison to all the shifters in the country, and he worked with the government in their favor, creating laws and amendments that benefited their people. She wanted to be a part of that, and finally, she would be. She couldn't wait to start her new job next week.

Tonight was the first time she'd been to a huge Motsi event in years. She'd gone to small parties here and there when she came home to visit, but she had been serious about her school work. Now that she had her dream job, she had planned to change her lifestyle, and these big events weren't on the list. Except, in exchange for her father helping her land her new job, he required her presence at her parent's side during the more significant events. Julissa knew what that meant.

Micah Crespo was ready to marry off his only daughter.

She sighed and drank some more champagne. Her father hadn't said that in so many words, but the parade of eligible men started from the moment she'd stepped through the door. She assumed knowing her plans would be enough to deter her father, but alas. She looked around the crowded room, skimming the golden décor. The ballroom was teeming with power and crackling energy, the sound of the many conversations bouncing off the two-story ceiling. She needed a breather. But before she could get one, her mother pulled her closer and introduced someone else. Julissa pasted on a smile and held out her hand. His name ran into all the others, his promise to get in touch with her later the same. He stared at her in a way that was not at all flattering. She could almost hear coins pinging around in his head. Marrying Julissa came with a massive influx of money from her marriage trust, and this male was counting them already. She excused herself and took off for the balcony. If she were lucky, it would be empty.

She took her first deep breath of the cool night air, and the most intoxicating smell came with it. She whipped her body around, searching the large balcony for the source. Her bear wanted to lavish in that scent and roll in it. Citrus, a hint of pepper, and deep, dark, luscious vanilla laced the potent aroma.

It made her hungry…reckless.

She spotted him, or well, his silhouette, in the corner of two cement posts. His body was large and powerful. Her feet carried her closer. She didn't have a choice. Her bear was pushing her at this point. His form became clear once she entered the shadows with him, and her animal's night vision took over. His eyes glowed as he lifted his glass to sip. Intense. Julissa could think of no other word to describe his gaze. It seared through her, burning down any inhibitions she might have had.

Her mouth watered as her gaze traced his face. Strong jaw, high cheekbones, and dark, dark eyes, it was a face that would make anyone look twice. His tall, muscled body fit perfectly into a red tuxedo with an elegant, subtle, plaid pattern, the suit pants hugging his thighs. Tattoos crawled from the neck of his dress shirt right up to underneath the low-cut beard that covered his strong chin. His full lips were dark pink, begging for her to bite them. Waves covered the top of his head, faded into a taper cut on the sides.

He was…everything.

An air of danger surrounded him, her feminine instincts warning her that he may be more than she could handle, but she pushed that aside. She took a deep breath and tried to contain her racing heart. His gaze never left her as she perused his body.

Hers.

Juilssa's bear declared it, clawing at her insides for her to run to him. She was struck mute.

Where someone else would rush to fill in the silence, this male didn't. He sipped from his drink, his eyes never leaving hers. The tension rose between them, thickening the air. The years in the Motsi had made her a confident woman. Julissa had never had an issue conversing with anyone, but this man intimidated her. But simultaneously, her bear wanted to submit to him and curl under him.

She cleared her throat and fought to think of some kind of witty banter. Anything to break the weighted silence. She wanted...no needed to know who he was. Yeah, she could start with that. Before she could open her mouth to ask, he tilted his head as though listening before his lips lifted in a small taunting smile.

"They looking for you, sug."

His voice.

That deep, gravelly sound seemed to scrape over her skin, pulling goosebumps in its wake. Who was he?

"Julissa!" her mother called for her on the other side of the balcony.

Her heartbeat thundered. Fear that she would

lose this man and this moment made panic flare within her.

"Go, mama. We'll meet again."

Confident. Reassuring. His words loosened her feet, and she moved to answer her mother's call. But not before one more glance at his face. Julissa burned it into her memory. Yeah, they would meet again. She would make sure of it.

ROCCO WATCHED THE FEMALE, Julissa, as she left the balcony. She left behind a scent that would haunt him and his bear. It was deep, sensual amber layered on top of a bright, floral magnolia. He committed it to memory, knowing he would make well on his promise to her. It wouldn't be hard to find her. Everyone knew Julissa Crespo. Her father was a powerful man in Eastfield. One who was very protective of his daughter. Not that that would stop Rocco. His bear wanted to chase her down now, but he had other pressing matters to handle at the moment. To that end, his phone buzzed with an address.

He waited until enough time had elapsed before he left the balcony. He didn't want even the slightest hint of impropriety to hit her. He wanted her, yes, but he had no plans for anyone to know that. If he was lucky, he and his bear could get their fill of her, and she would still be eligible to be mated afterward. His bear bucked in denial, but Rocco squashed it. They couldn't keep her, no matter what part of him longed to do so. They weren't fit for her. Adina Knight spotted him the moment he re-entered the ballroom.

"Rocco," she looped her arm in his. "I have some people I want you to meet."

"Mama Di." He warned.

She waved off his protest. "I got my other boys mated off; it's your turn."

He grunted and shook his head. Mating wasn't in the cards for him. He could tell her that, but it would go in one ear and out the other. From the moment her son had brought him home, Adina Knight had been mothering him. If she had her way, Rocco would've been adopted into their family and living under their roof. Despite all the therapy she'd made him get, Rocco adamantly held himself separate from them, at least as much as they would allow.

"Silas is mated, and it's time for you to stop following him everywhere and settle down."

"I'm his security. It's my job to follow him everywhere."

She sucked her teeth. "Please. You could've been handed that over to Theo. You can work at any one of the garages you own."

He shrugged because even if he weren't protecting Silas, them people would barely see him. He spent his off time at the garage closest to his house because it specialized in vintage car restoration, and he used it to work on his own car. Adina was right. It and the others he owned made him enough money that he could quit working for Silas. But…he owed his best friend his life.

Literally.

It had been Silas who had found him on the street stealing money to feed himself. The day he met Silas, his whole life had changed.

From the corner of his eye, he spotted Julissa. She was surrounded by her friends, smiling. The brightness of that smile reached down inside of him and warmed him. His bear rumbled. What would it be like to have that sunshine aimed at him? He memorized her face, from her large doe eyes surrounded by lush lashes to her button nose and full-painted lips. Her strong jaw and high cheekbones gave her a regal appearance. Her blood-red velvet gown made her pecan brown skin glow and clung to curves that made his mouth water. She was temptation come to life. His heart thumped hard against his chest.

It wasn't for him.

"Ma, I gotta handle something tonight, so rain check on the matchmaking," he rumbled.

"Liar," Adina chided. "Fine. But I'm not giving up, despite your stubbornness."

"Noted," he teased and nuzzled against her cheek.

He walked away and sought out her son. He found Silas where he'd left him last, whispering in his mate's ear. The two made a striking couple. The natural and affectionate way they handled each other showcased their love to anyone who saw them. Silas was a different man than he'd been before he found his family, and Rocco loved that for him.

"I need to head out," he told his friend. "Theo is circulating and close."

Silas looked up, his eyes sharp. "What's going on?"

"A potential tenant."

"Be careful, Rock. Text me when you get home."

"I'm good."

Silas narrowed his eyes. "You going by your-self?"

"Deena's meeting me there."

"Bet. See you Sunday."

They dapped up, and Rock made his way to the exit. He felt eyes on him as he got close to the door. He turned and met Julissa's gaze. She licked her lips, and a shudder of want moved through his body. She was beautiful, and though he knew he couldn't keep her for himself, for a moment, he was tempted. He gave her a small salute and left the room before he could be put off his task.

Two

He knew it would happen.

He kept his body still as his heart raced, thumping in his chest in an erratic staccato rhythm. The metallic scent of his fear filled the room, slowly dissipating as Rocco returned to himself and finally escaped the last vestiges of the nightmare. Every time he got a new tenant. Every time he saw the devastated looks on the faces of their children, the nightmares returned. It was understandable. The pain and uncertainty in the cubs' eyes were so similar to the dead look he used to have in his so many years ago.

Rocco brought his trembling hand up to his face squeezing the bridge of his nose as he calmed his breathing. His cellphone buzzed next to him on the bedside table, reminding him of what had awakened him. He squinted at the clock and sighed. It was barely six, but Deena never called him with trivial shit. She knew him too well for that.

"Yeah," he finally answered the buzzing device.

"Sorry, it's so early. I finally got 2B settled. The shelter called at five this morning." Deena hurriedly said.

"They need anything?"

His mind went to the small puma shifter he'd had to rescue last night. She had been in bad shape by the time he'd arrived at the small rundown house where the female had been staying with her abusive mate and two children. The coward had run off, and the woman had finally reached out to the women's shelter, where his friend Deena volunteered. He'd dropped the family off and let Deena handle the rest. He knew that sometimes his presence could set off the females, but he never allowed his friend to travel alone by herself that time of night. He made a small note to let Dallas's office know about the family.

"Rock?" Deena said softly.

It took his mind off the memory of the puma's children and back to the conversation at hand.

He sighed. "I'm good."

"Are you sure? I know how these cases set you off."

"Good, D." He assured her, rolling out of bed. Going back to sleep would be impossible.

"I was going to try and talk you into leasing the other vacant apartments, but last night was hard. I'll let it go for now."

He grunted. He didn't like his building too full. He never regretted helping the families, but he liked his peace.

"It's a good thing you're doing, Rocco. Let that soothe the wounds," she told him gently.

"I'll try," he lied.

She sucked her teeth, seeing through it as she always did. They'd done this dance for years. The group home where they'd spent the last years of their teenage life had made them close.

"I'll check on you later."

"I'm good, Deena. No need to mother me," He growled out.

She didn't get offended at his broken voice, only chuckling. "Fine. Later, grumpy."

He hung up the phone and headed to his shower. He turned the spray to hot, stepping in while it was still cold. It didn't take the water long to heat to scalding. He let the pain wash over him for long minutes before finally relenting and turning it down. The heat never matched the fires of hell that the dream thrust him into.

The drive over to Silas's house was done in silence. He probably should've at least turned the radio on, but the noise would just agitate his bear more. He parked in the driveway and sighed before leaving the car. He fixed his face into an affable expression that would hopefully hide his anxiety from his best friend and family. After composing himself, Rock opened the front door and was greeted with the typical cacophony of sound that now lived permanently in Silas's house.

"Uncle Rock!" Sariyah jumped into his arms, her school uniform halfway tucked.

"Morning, Poppet," he greeted, settling her down on her feet. He could tell from her mother's flustered expression that they were likely running late this morning.

"Oh, good. Hold him for a sec," Mila breathed

out, thrusting her six-month-old son Carter into his arms.

He cuddled the infant, smiling as Carter grabbed his cheeks, slobbering and babbling. He growled, and Carter dive-bombed into his chest to get closer to the sound. Rock took his first easy breath of the morning as he held his nephew. Mila looked up from where she was making little swoopy things with the edges of Riyah's hair and smiled.

"He loves his Uncle Rock. Look at him," she chuckled.

"I thought y'all had to be to school early today," Silas commented, coming down the stairs.

Mila sighed and grabbed Carter out of Rock's arms. "We're getting there."

Silas leaned down and kissed his mate and daughter, nuzzling his son. "We're gone, then. I love you."

Rock smiled at his friend and the happiness he'd found. That happiness had managed to rub off on him, his best friend's family bringing him joy when he'd long thought he wouldn't have any. He walked Silas out to the blacked-out SUV Rock drove when he was guarding him. His friend studied him as he buckled into the seat.

"What's up with you?"

"Nothing," Rock said, backing out of the drive-way.

And for the most part, it was now true. Just spending that little bit of time with his niece and nephew had improved his mood.

"How did last night go?" Silas asked.

Rock tensed before grunting.

"You do what you can, Rock."

He nodded, reminding himself that that had to be enough.

Three

Julissa Crespo took a deep breath, staring at the imposing building that housed the Tri-council and the many other essential offices that dealt with the health and safety of the Motsi. She'd been here before, but only as the youngest child and only daughter to Councilman Micah Crespo. She'd played in those same halls that she would now walk as an adult and an employee. It had been one of the privileges of her father's position.

She was twenty-five, fresh out of law school, and ready to use that privilege to help the shifters in their town. If it were up to her mother, she'd have left college with her MRS and been married to the wealthiest, most powerful shifter her parents could arrange. But she'd wanted different.

Her new job was one she was looking forward

to. Yes, her father had gotten her the job, but damn it, she would prove she deserved it. Taking a deep breath and slipping her Chanel bag over her shoulder, she headed towards the security check-in, ready to take on the day. Her designer heels clicked against the pavement, and she counted her steps, using the sound to calm her nerves. She went through security quickly, her face one they were used to seeing in the building. Pushing through the glass doors of Silas Knight's office had her hands trembling.

His staff was small, just four other shifters who did the research and work that went into crafting the bills and amendments that were eventually turned into laws protecting shifters across the country. Ever since the war with the humans, the shifters had kept themselves separate. Each state had its own governing system, but most adopted the tri-council method. The Shifter Liason's position worked with all those councils to meet the needs of all the shifters in the country. It was a huge undertaking.

She was giddy with excitement. Silas's assistant looked up, smiling at her. Julissa talked to Keisha last week when she learned that her father had successfully gotten her on the staff. She hoped Keisha's easy demeanor was the same with all the staff. She didn't know how they would treat her, knowing nepotism had gotten her the job.

"Hi, Julissa! Welcome aboard." Keisha greeted, standing. The bright jade pantsuit contrasted with the woman's beautiful light skin and reassured Julissa that she hadn't over-dressed.

Julissa held out her hand. "I'm so happy to be here."

"Come on. I have a desk ready for you and a ton of paperwork for you to fill out. I'll get you a badge, though I'm sure you'll never have an issue getting into the building."

"You have no idea how excited I'll be to flash a badge, though." Julissa joked.

Keisha laughed, giving her a warm look. "Well, let's get you started. You have a meeting with Silas at ten. It's a simple meet and greet where he'll run down your duties. You're fresh from law school, so it'll be mostly researching."

Julissa nodded because Keisha had gone over that information with her when they spoke over the phone. Within the next few minutes, Julissa was settled into her new desk with a pile of papers to go through. She took a deep breath to settle her nerves and got down to it.

Julissa flexed her fingers as she filled out yet another NDA. Keisha had said there would be forms, but good God almighty, she had undersold it. Her bear moved through her body, and she froze, inhaling deeply, tilting her head in confusion. The animal was tense, the alertness warning her that something was coming.

She inhaled again, and her bear rolled over in her chest, making it flutter. She recognized that smell. Her eyes scanned the office, brushing over the employees that had been here when she'd arrived. None of the five people had elicited even a smidge of curiosity from the animal. Her bear knew the owner of that scent and was begging her to get up and find it.

He'd promised to meet her again. Was she finally getting her chance?

"You ready?" Keisha asked, stepping into Julissa's line of sight.

Clearing her face, Julissa nodded, standing and

brushing her hand down the red wide-legged trousers she was wearing. She slid her arms into the matching jacket, covering the black blouse. She nervously followed Keisha, her bear getting more active the closer they got to Silas's office. Once his door was open, the elusive scent was like a hammer. There was only Silas Knight in the office, so she was confused. He was mated, so her bear dismissed the male quickly, scanning his office for the source of that heavenly smell.

The bear shifter from Sunday night stood in the corner of the room. His arms were crossed over his chest, his dark eyes intent and laser-focused on her. Her body ignited, and longing filled her. He was here! Instead of the red tux, she'd first seen him in, his muscular body was covered in all black—from the fitted slacks to the dress shirt he wore opened to the top of his chest. A whole fucking snack.

"Julissa, hi." Silas stood and extended his hand. "Long time no see."

She tore her eyes from the male and focused on her new boss. "College and then law school kept me away."

"Of course," he said, sitting back in his chair.

"Do you remember my best friend, Rocco?" He indicated the male in the corner.

She frowned. This was Rocco Jamison? She'd heard of him. He was feared all over the city. His name alone kept Silas Knight safe in most instances. This was the male her bear had chosen? Even without consulting the animal, there was no mistake. She was drawn to him.

She nodded to Rocco and turned her gaze back to Silas, almost positive she would embarrass herself if she kept staring. Her palms were sweaty as the realization of what Rocco was to her rained down on her.

Her father would throw a fit if she mated with him. Her bear bucked. Ok, no if...when? But that would all be dependent on him. She was afraid to look at him. But everything in her was yearning for him. When she finally got up the courage to look him in his face again, the heat in his eyes took her breath away. Rocco was staring at her intently. She felt like she could see her future with him. It made her feel amazing. She knew she would fight her whole family for a chance with this man.

Four

Rocco stared at the door of Silas's office, his bear bucking against his skin. He'd finally sat back down, his leg bouncing as what just happened washed over him. His bear had been restless all morning, but Rocco had ignored the animal. Julissa spent a lot of time with her father in this building, so he brushed aside her distracting scent earlier. He was operating on about three hours of sleep and could ill afford another distraction. Protecting Silas would take every ounce of his waning attention span today.

At least, that's what he'd thought.

Now, he understood his bear's restlessness. The animal had probably clocked her presence hours ago. Where he was sleepy just minutes ago, nervous energy pinged through him. Just her presence had done that. What would it be like when he finally had her? His bear was talking reckless, sending out signals of her being theirs, but he'd already reconciled himself with just having a taste of her.

"When did you hire her?"

Silas smiled and inhaled, his eyebrows shooting up. "I didn't see you with a pampered princess." He ignored Rock's question.

Rocco growled. "Not too much."

Silas outright laughed. "Wait until I tell Mase. You better tell Dallas Knight before he finds out from the streets."

Rocco sucked his teeth. "What streets? You?"

His friend simply smiled and went back to his work. "You already know I'm finna tell my baby, and she gon' tell CiCi, and then...."

He groaned because the Knight family was tight as hell. They didn't keep secrets from each other, and as Silas reminded him, they considered him family, so his life was fodder for their meddling. His eyes went back to the door.

Julissa Crespo.

His bear had to be tripping. He wanted her with a need that frankly scared him. Silas was right; she was a pampered princess. A darling of the Motsi society and way too good for him. He licked his lips, inhaling deep before the bright notes of her scent faded. She was built like most sows. The female bear-shifters all had those wide, luscious hips and thick thighs. Her deep red pants accentuated her waist, giving her a coke bottle shape. His mouth watered.

"Councilman Crespo won't allow it."

He hadn't meant to say that aloud, but now that the words were out, he realized how true they were. Besides, he had no plans to mate with the woman. He wanted one…maybe ten nights with her. Surely that would be enough to get her out of his system.

"Fuck her daddy. He can't come between mates." Silas didn't even look up from his work.

"I'm not mating."

That got his friend's attention. Silas looked up with a frown. "Rock. I can feel your bear from over here. No way that girl ain't yours."

Rocco shrugged. She didn't deserve to be saddled with him.

Silas sighed. "So you plan to what, have an affair with her?" He snorted. "Yeah right."

"That's all I can offer her," he murmured.

"Bullshit." Silas snapped. "But I'll let you make it. Your animal don't give a fuck what you talking about anyway."

"She's too young."

Silas grunted but didn't answer. Rocco had to be at least ten years older than her. Would that matter to Julissa? Maybe if he intended to mate her, it would matter. But for an affair, surely it wouldn't. He debated his first steps, ignoring his animal for now.

For once in his life, Rocco was glad that it was Friday. It had been the longest week of his life. All week, Julissa's presence tortured him. Silas's words had haunted him during the day as he watched her, and at night, dreams of what he would do kept him up. He was down bad. He'd never thought about what he would do if he met his mate. As far as he was concerned, he'd never get that lucky, and if he did, he'd planned to ignore it. He hadn't understood the pull the mating call would have on him.

It was foolish to think he could have sex with her and discard her when he was done.

Naïve.

He'd never really made rounds in Silas' office before, but with Julissa there, he'd left his friend's office every few minutes to get a glimpse of her. He was still unsure whether he would do something about their mating. The age thing gave him pause, as well as her position in the Motsi society. He came with a lot of baggage.

He pulled the antique Chevy Nova he drove to work into the parking lot of his building. The four-story building had been Dallas' gift to him when he finished college. Rocco hadn't wanted to go, but Adina had been insistent, and there wasn't anything he could deny the woman. She'd all but adopted him, but he wouldn't let her take that last step.

At the time when she'd asked if he wanted them to adopt him officially, he told them no. He didn't want to forget his own mother and the shit she'd suffered to make his life possible. Adina hadn't taken offense, but she still showed up to his school for conferences and to chew him out when he and Silas had gotten into trouble. It wasn't just her either. Silas and Mason had treated him like their brother. In the first two garages he'd opened, the two had been next to him, gutting the interiors and helping him flip the warehouse space he'd bought into a pristine working space.

They'd cussed and fussed about it, but it hadn't stopped them or Julian from showing up every weekend. He had meant to eventually flip this apartment building, but he hadn't been able to part with it. He'd diligently worked on it until he was able to rent out the apartments.

He and Deena worked with the local women's shelter to find tenants. He wanted a place for the women to go that would be safe for their children and allow them the space to get back on their feet. So far, he and Deena had helped many women, and he was proud of that. It enabled him to honor his mother's memory.

He frowned as he spotted the blacked-out Range Rover idling in front of his building. His doorman knew damn well better than that. He got out of his car and took in the scents of the night. He frowned at the familiar scent. He sucked his teeth when he realized why it was partially recognizable. He knew the familial scent to match very well. It was someone kin to Julissa, and if rumors were correct, more than likely her brothers.

The doors to the truck opened as he got closer, and the two bulky males exited the truck, leaning against the hood as they waited for him. Lachlan and Liam Crespo were paying him a visit. Wasn't he lucky? The two men were identical, their six-five height and heavy bodies made to intimidate. Their skin was darker than their sisters, their sharp features a mirror of their father's. They were dressed in all black, and Rock could only assume it was supposed to scare him or some shit.

He shook his head, not even bothering to let them get under his skin. "Get from in front my spot like this. Shit looks janky," he rumbled.

"We came to talk."

He didn't know which of them spoke, and he didn't give a damn. He eyed them because, from the way the twins were squeezing their hands, talking was the last thing they came to do. He crossed his arms over his chest.

"Say your speech and get the fuck on."

They growled and moved closer in tandem. Rock didn't move an inch because ain't shit he feared out here.

"Our sister has been asking around about you. We want you to leave her alone."

"No," he said calmly.

The fuck he look like letting someone scare him off his mate? He'd had no plans on claiming her, but just the thought of someone coming between him and his potential mate riled his bear and had him changing his mind. So, against his better judgment and despite a week's worth of fighting, Rocco would claim his mate. A petty way to decide, yes, he could admit that. But the animal wouldn't allow anyone between them. His bear filled his body to drive that point home.

"You know who the fuck we are, Rock."

"I can say the same." He told them, and they frowned.

Before Dallas had made his way into the Motsi, he and Silas stayed in shit and had a reputation that had preceded the family's ascension into society. While Silas had cleaned up his act to maintain his current position, Rock hadn't seen the point. Besides, he did the same stuff he'd been doing in the streets, except now for the family's protection.

"We can make this conversation more painful if necessary." One twin warned.

Rocco smirked and shook his head, walking around them. He might have taken them up on that any other night, but now that he'd decided to pursue Julissa, dragging her brothers across his parking lot would likely not endear her to him.

"Julissa is promised to someone else."

He didn't slow his pace towards the door, though the words struck him right in the chest. He would kill anyone who even thought to take her from him. Damn, it. Silas had been right. His bear didn't care about any of that shit he was talking about earlier. None of his reasonings mattered to his animal.

"She's mine. Tell him to find something safe to do with himself," he told them over his shoulder.

They growled louder as Rocco gave them his back and walked inside.

The night doorman stood abruptly. "I already tried—"

Rock waved him off. "Next time, call back up."

He nodded. "Yes, sir."

He turned and stared at her brothers, dropping his fangs in a warning. He had no problems getting active if the situation called for it. Shooting him an aggravated look, the twins got in the truck and drove off. Rock already knew he would hear about it. He went to his apartment and sighed. The last thing he wanted was beef with a tri-council member about his daughter, but Julissa was non-negotiable.

He had barely gotten out of the shower when his phone rang. He shook his head when he saw the number.

"Sup, PD."

"The councilman's daughter, Rocco?"

He chuckled at Dallas's tone. "I'm being respectful."

Dallas sighed. "What we doing?"

"She's my mate." He told Dallas. His bear finally relaxed, hearing the man claim her out loud.

"I'll handle it then."

He grunted, already knowing Dallas would have his back.

"Her brothers ain't wrapped tight, though, so they may still come at you about their baby sister," he warned.

"I ain't worried."

Dallas chuckled. "Alright then, that's all I needed to know. You remember what I told you about heat?"

Rocco grunted. He remembered the very detailed information Dallas had given them all about sex and mating when they hit puberty. Bears differed from panthers, but PD ensured Rocco had gotten information specific to his animal. It was one of many small ways the Knights had shown him that he was a part of their family.

"DiDi and Iris know, so you already know what will happen on Sunday."

Lord have mercy.

He pinched the bridge of his nose. "PD."

"My name is Bennet, and I ain't in it." Dallas laughed, hanging up the phone.

He hadn't even made moves on Julissa, and already gossip was flying around Eastfield.

Five

Julissa rolled her shoulders and maneuvered around the boxes scattered across her new apartment. She'd been in the place for two months and made no moves to unpack. There were two bedrooms, and she planned to use one of them as her closet. Or at least she would when she got around to organizing all her clothes. Right now, they were carefully stored in wardrobe boxes. She finished tying off the silk scarf that covered her hair and headed for the kitchen.

She shoved boxes of kitchen stuff to the side. She didn't cook, so she hadn't seen the need to rush and unpack those. Besides, with her new job, she would barely have the time. She was in awe of Silas Knight, she'd seen him from afar and studied so many of his bills and case law, but nothing had prepared her for how hard he and his staff worked. It was exhilarating being a part of it. The Motsi was supposed to help shifters, and for so long, she'd felt like they hadn't been doing enough. She wanted to do more, help more, and now she could do that.

A month and a half in, and yes, the hours were long and the details tedious, but she was excited all the same. Now, if she could just get her hormones under control. She had to work in the same office as Rocco daily, and he had yet to approach her. Her bear insisted that he was her mate, but damn if she could work up the courage to say something to him. Just like the night she'd first seen him, he had her tongue-tied.

It hadn't stopped her from asking around about him. She wanted to know as much about him as she could. She'd hoped it would help her step to him, but she'd chickened out so far. For the last week, though, she'd noticed little gifts left on her desk, covered in his scent. She didn't know how to take that. His promise that night on the balcony had fueled many of her dreams about him. Julissa was waiting impatiently for him to ask her out. Though she appreciated having her favorite lunch delivered to her desk, she wanted to eat those lunches with him. Off him.

She shuddered at the need that slammed into her. Just thinking about the man made her hot. When was he going to make his move?

Julissa sighed in frustration and sucked her teeth at the sad state of the refrigerator. Once again, she'd forgotten to grocery shop. She slapped a sandwich together with the measly fixings she found, too tired and hungry to wait on takeout. She frowned when her phone rang. It was the front door of her building.

She sighed when she saw her mother and her detail hovering around her doorbell camera. Julissa pushed the button to let them in and waited. A few minutes later, she heard the beep of the keypad as her mother let herself in, leaving her detail in the hallway.

Therese Crespo was everything one could expect for a society maven. The graceful woman was well into her fifties, but her caramel brown skin glowed smooth and unwrinkled due to her meticulous care. Her hair was back in a low chignon, with tendrils surrounding her beautiful face. Therese was her version of 'dressed down.' Tailor-fitted cream-colored slacks hugged her ample curves, and the white silk blouse on top opened to her collar. The cashmere sweater worn on top was one her mother had owned for as long as Julissa could remember. According to Therese, it was Micah's first gift to his mate, and she cherished it.

"Mom," she greeted around the sandwich she was eating.

"Julissa, really." Therese looked around her apartment and sighed. "I could've had this all done for you. Why do you insist on living like you're still in the dorms?"

"Mom, my apartment is fine. I'll get to it eventually."

Her mother sat her purse down on the counter and looked around. "I see you managed to unpack your bookshelf and set up your reading nook," she said drolly.

"The important stuff." she joked.

Therese stared at her only daughter.

Julissa sighed. "What did they say?"

She knew that look on her mother's face. Either her father or brothers were complaining about something she'd done. She racked her mind for what kind of trouble she could've gotten into in the last month. She'd kept her head down and worked, so she couldn't imagine what sacred breach of safety she'd violated. She hadn't even attempted to lose the detail her father had put on her in that time. And she certainly hadn't had time to attend any Motsi events. Her friends had been nagging her for the last week about it.

"Liam and Lachlan are under the impression that you're mated."

Julissa frowned, though her heart thumped a little in guilt. What did she even say to that? "Mom, seriously."

Therese shrugged and opened one of the kitchen boxes. She started putting away the fancy dishes that Julissa had never had a reason to use, but Therese had insisted she needed.

"I'm just relaying."

"I'm not mated."

Therese eyed her but carried on with her task. "So, who has your brothers and father so worried?"

"What are they worried about? I go to work, and I come home. The not-so-secret detail dad has on me can attest to that."

Therese nodded, not bothering to deny that her husband kept tabs on their only daughter. "There is clearly someone, Julissa. Your father was in a screaming match with Dallas Knight a couple of weeks ago, and you know Micah never yells."

Her eyes widened. "Mom, I swear I haven't mated behind your backs."

Therese turned and put a hand on her hip. She pointed to her daughter. "See that? See how careful you are with your words. Who is he?"

She sighed and gave up on the rest of her sandwich. "I...we have barely exchanged more than a few words. Why in the world do the twins think anything is going on?"

Julissa bit her lip. Perhaps she'd not been as discreet as she thought when asking around about Rocco.

Therese huffed and moved to the next box.

"Mom, you don't have to do that. I can do it when I get ready to."

"I'm here, and you know I can't just sit around in mess."

Julissa sighed and took that gentle rebuke for what it was. "Mom," she put her head down on the counter.

"You know the plans your father had for you,

sweetheart. Just spit it out so I can fix it. I need peace in my house, child."

Julissa straightened, "Mama."

"Aht-aht, don't even, Julissa Nicole, out with it."

"His name is Rocco Jamison."

Therese's eyebrows shot up. "Rocco Jamison. I see. That explains your father and Dallas. He's older than you, baby."

That didn't matter to her. She would have him. "I don't want to start anything with Daddy's allies."

Therese waved that away. "I'll talk to Adina, and the two of us will fix it. You can't leave it to men to do anything but measure their dicks."

Julissa snorted. "He's my mate, but we haven't even…."

Therese walked to her daughter, cupping her cheek. "An actual mate, Julissa? Not just a man you want to marry?"

She nodded.

Her mother gave her a happy, watery smile and backed away, returning to the boxes. "I'm happy for you, love. I prefer a mating to any match your father could make for you."

"I wouldn't be too happy yet. Rocco doesn't even talk to me. He just…" she sighed. "He leaves me gifts and buys me lunch, but he's not making a move."

Therese smiled. "Bear mates are different, sweetheart. They have to make sure you're receptive before they make a move. Have you even looked up from work to let him know?"

She frowned. "You see what happens when I show even a smidge of interest in a man."

Therese sighed. "Liam and Lachlan are worse than your father. They even went to his apartment to scare him off the other day. Probably another reason your father and Dallas got into it."

She growled, aggravated. "Mom."

Therese shrugged. "You know how they are. I rein them in where I can."

Julissa could only sigh because her mother was right. Therese had fought for her to be able to leave the state for college. Every time she needed her mother, she was there backing her up when her brothers and father ganged up on her.

"What did they say to Rocco?"

Therese gave her a droll look, and her stomach churned. Julissa needed to go over there and clean up her brothers' mess. She looked down at the t-shirt and tights she wore. She needed to change clothes first. She wondered briefly how she could speed up her mother's visit. She already knew where he lived. That had been one of the more complicated pieces of information to get, but gossip was hard to escape in the Motsi, and everything about the Knights and the people they'd brought with them to the society was fodder for it.

That included where her mate laid his head.

"Forget them for the moment. Tell me about him." Therese ordered.

"Rocco is...stoic," she searched for a better word. "How do I let him know I'm receptive, Mom?" She asked softly.

Therese smiled. "Well, sweetheart. Let me tell you about trapping a bear."

Six

Rocco slid a pair of joggers up his leg, his bear still restless within his body. He'd upped time in his animal form, running for an hour, but the damned beast was pushing. He knew what his bear wanted, but he was going at his pace and wouldn't be rushed. Lowkey still didn't even think he deserved his mate, so the fact that he was making moves at all should've satisfied the animal. To that end, he picked up his phone off the bed and scrolled through the florist's website he'd been perusing before he'd gotten into the shower.

He frowned when the intercom near his door rang. Slipping his phone into his pocket, he pressed the button. The face of his doorman appeared.

"There's a Julissa Crespo here to see you."

Rocco cursed, and his bear bucked in excitement. "Send her up."

He looked around, but there was nothing to clean. He kept his apartment sparse, and now wished he'd put in more effort. The apartment details were meticulous and luxurious, from the crown molding and gold lighting fixtures to the hand-laid hardwood floors. He had done the built-ins himself, making his place look not as empty...but still. There was a sofa and his massive tv mounted on the wall. That's it. What would his mate think?

She knocked a minute later, and he took a deep breath before opening the door. He'd seen her just two hours ago as she was leaving the office, and still, her presence hit him in the chest. He drank her in. She was so beautiful and elegant. She wore a soft, thick sweater dress that hugged her frame from neck to ankle, though it left her arms exposed. It made him want to rub against her.

"Hi, Rocco," she said softly.

He inclined his head, and she entered his space. His bear rumbled his chest triumphantly, but he squashed the animal before it got carried away.

She was only here for…whatever she had come for. He inhaled, indulging in her scent.

"Have you eaten?"

Where the fuck had that come from?

She shook her head. "Whatever you're making smells amazing." She turned from her perusal of his space, giving him a small smile.

The fish he'd put in the oven before he jumped in the shower should be near done. There was enough for him to share, but even if it weren't, he'd have given it all to her. He didn't say anything, simply pointing to the stool at the kitchen island. He turned off the rice cooker and pulled down plates for them.

"Do you need any help?" She broke the silence.

He shook his head. He didn't speak much on most days, but the people who knew him were used to it. He'd always been subconscious about his rough voice. His tattoos easily covered the scars on his neck, but that gravelly rumbling had never healed, which was odd for shifters, but he'd been injured prior to getting his animal, so he was stuck with the damage his father had caused. He shook the morbid thoughts from his head and focused his attention back on Julissa. He didn't want to scare her off with his brooding.

He plated their food and placed hers in front of her.

She smiled up at him. "This smells amazing. Thank you for sharing. I know I dropped by unexpectedly."

He nodded and sat down next to her. She grabbed his hand, praying over their food. That small act settled his whole body. It was like everything he'd been missing in his life clicked into place with her presence in his den. She finished and dug in, moaning at the first taste. He closed his eyes to keep his bear from showing its ass. He already loved feeding her, but to know she enjoyed food directly from his hand was an experience he didn't realize would mean so much.

"This is amazing," she gushed. "Do you cook like this all the time?"

He cleared the lump from his throat and carefully modulated his voice. "Not all the time."

"Don't do that," she said, touching his shoulder. "You don't have to adjust your voice for me."

He stared at her, and she squirmed, pulling her bottom lip between her teeth.

"I'm sorry. Did I overstep?"

He shook his head and went back to his food. She pushed her green beans around on her plate, and what was once a comfortable silence shifted. She pushed out a breath and straightened her shoulders.

"So…I came over to apologize.

He frowned in question.

"About my brothers," she rushed out.

He tilted his head for her to go on, and she sighed.

"They're massively overprotective and don't have any home training."

A small chuckle escaped him, and she smiled. His chest tightened at her beauty. They stared at each other, the tension thickening between them for long moments. She licked her lips and cleared her throat.

"So, yeah. I'm sorry."

"You good. They did what they were supposed to do."

She squinted her eyes. "You're one of those overprotective shifters, too?" She sighed dramatically. "Just my luck. Gonna spend my life like my mom with a cadre of security."

She seemed to realize what she had said, and her eyes widened in horror. Multiple expressions flitted across her face, easy to read. She was amusing, her sweetness and light filling him, relaxing him and his bear.

"I mean…I didn't mean…like, I was just…" she blinked, her face shocked and unsure.

JULISSA WANTED TO sink through the floor. She shared one dinner with the man and was already envisioning her life with him. What was wrong with her?

She tried again. "Rocco, I…"

The corner of his lip tilted up in what she assumed was a small smile. "You good, Liss."

He returned to his food, and she waited, but he didn't say anything else. She let out a relieved breath when he didn't fill the silence. Stoic. That's what she'd told her mother about him, which was clearly true. He was a man of few words.

She hid her smile as she took another bite of food. Liss. She liked that. It sounded even more remarkable coming out of his mouth. She'd never had a nickname before. Even her friends of years called her Julissa. No one had shortened her name.

"You must've just moved into your apartment,"

she prodded, taking another look around the empty place.

It would be a great space once he decorated it. The sizeable airy apartment was calling for lush plants and wild splashes of color, at least if she lived here. Lord, Julissa shook her head. She was already moving into his place, and the man had yet to ask her out on a date.

"At least you don't have boxes everywhere like me. My mom was just fussing at me about the state of my apartment."

He hummed, which said nothing.

"The building is nice. I wonder if they have any apartments available." Not one to take silence, she rushed to fill it, which explained why she kept her foot in her mouth around this man. "I don't mean I'm going to move down the hallway from you. Like, I'm not gonna run down to the leasing office. Just…"

She shoved food in her mouth, hoping that would keep her from saying something else goofy.

Rocco grunted. "I own the building."

Her eyes widened. "Oh, that's so cool! How many apartments…" she trailed off because she was finna sound full-on unhinged if she kept going.

Why did he make her so nervous!?

He chuckled. "Six."

"Oh."

She was scared to say anything else after that. They ate in silence for a few minutes, but the way her mouth was set up…

"Thank you for the lunches and the flowers." She said.

He nodded. "I like feeding you. Spoiling you."

Her stomach fluttered, her bear melting with her. She waited for Rocco to expand his sweet words, but he didn't, which made his succinct statement that much more potent. Her body flushed. They ate dinner not quite in silence because she would never be what someone would call quiet. He didn't seem to mind, though, simply humming to show he was listening, answering any questions she asked in one-word sentences when required. When they finished eating, Julissa sought a reason to prolong her visit. But she probably wore out her welcome, especially since she hadn't asked to come over. So, she stood and gathered their dishes.

"I can clean up."

He stopped her with a hand on her arm. She

put the plates back down. He turned on the stool and pulled her between his legs.

"I'll handle it."

"It's the least I can do since I made you share your dinner. We can go out for dessert. I'm sure your bear is still hungry," she rambled.

He smiled, a full one that lit his face, and Julissa's world tilted. She had never seen him smile this big. It relaxed his face and made him approachable. Her hand skimmed his cheek before she realized what she was doing.

"You have a beautiful smile," she said softly.

He licked his lips and nuzzled into her hand. "Thank you for coming over."

"Are you kicking me out?" she teased.

He chuckled softly. "I'm trying to behave and starting to lose my resolve."

Her stomach clenched, moisture gathering at her center. Rocco hissed and inhaled, his eyes darkening.

"See..." He shook his head and dropped his hands from her hips. "We finna get in trouble if you stay. Did you drive?"

She nodded, nervous and heated at his closeness. She was damn near salivating at his words.

Why couldn't she stay? She would love to get in trouble with him. Her bear was fully with it. He seemed to read her mind, chuckling, grabbing her hips, and bringing her back into him.

"At first...I thought I could separate what my bear wanted from what I wanted." His gaze traced her face slowly.

She held her breath, unsure what that meant. She wanted to ask, but he so rarely talked that she was afraid to break the moment.

His lips quirked up into a slight smirk. "In this, I think I'll listen to my animal."

"What does that mean?" she whispered.

"It means I could never be satisfied with having you once or twice." His other hand spanned her hip, bringing her closer to him. "We'll do this right. Can't have your daddy crying foul," he said softly, cupping her cheek.

He stood to his full height, and she looked up, swallowing the moan that wanted to escape at his touch. Her stomach clenched, and her heart raced. He effortlessly put her under his spell. She held her breath as his head descended, closing the distance between their faces.

"Good night, sug." He kissed her softly.

She closed her eyes to savor it, whimpering when he pulled back. "Good night, Rocco."

He separated from her and went to the coat rack at his door, pulling a hoodie over his t-shirt. Rocco walked her all the way downstairs and to her car. He nodded to the security her father had on her. It reminded her of his words about her daddy crying foul. He was right; her father would want a marriage contract before the two of them mated. For the first time in Julissa's life, her family's position in society felt stifling, especially since it was keeping her from her mate.

He held her door open until she buckled in, leaning down into her car.

"Gimme your phone, Liss." He ordered softly. She did, and he put in his number. "Text me as soon as you get home. Not in the parking lot, but inside your apartment safe."

She sucked her teeth in amusement. Yeah, Rocco would be overprotective. "Yes, daddy."

"Now see," he growled, closing the distance between them. He kissed her hard before pulling back and nipping her bottom lip. He stepped back and closed her door. "Behave."

She heard him through the closed window. Her

heart was racing, and her panties soaked. Would she be able to wait until he worked out a marriage contract with her father before she jumped him? Time would tell. Either way, her visit had been a success. Rocco had made his intentions for her clear. Satisfaction filled her. From the moment she'd entered society as a teenager, she understood that whom she married would be outside her control. But now, she would be mated and to someone she and her animal had chosen. Julissa squealed in happiness.

Seven

Julissa squirmed in her seat and fought not to check her phone for the fiftieth time since she'd arrived. It was Sunday brunch, and she was supposed to use this time to catch up with her friends. It was the first one she'd attended in months. Her friends were eager to see her. She was back from law school, and they wanted her to return to the social scene immediately. She loved Motsi events but was serious about her career; not all her old friends understood that. They were spoiled, all of them, her included, so most of them hadn't planned on working.

They would go straight from their father's homes to their husband or mate's, whichever came first.

"You've missed so much while you were gone," Keara started as soon as they were seated.

Julissa gave up her inner battle and took her phone out of her purse, setting it on the table in case Rocco texted her. They had been communicating and flirting a little since the dinner at his place. She followed her mother's advice and let him know she was open to their relationship, which seemed to work.

"Can you believe mousy little Celine Harris is mated and had a baby?" Keara whined.

Julissa rolled her eyes behind the menu. She'd been friends with all of these women since they were in diapers. It was the way the Motsi operated. One had to socialize with the right kind of people in order to keep their traditions alive. She didn't know what Keara had against Celine, but it was tired. The woman never bothered anyone when she attended events.

"You still mad that he didn't choose you?" Amber asked, snickering.

Keara glowered at her best friend, but Amber ignored her. Julissa was relieved when the waitress arrived with their pitcher. Bottomless mimosas were just what she needed.

"So, how do you like your new job?" Erica asked.

"It's great! Working with Silas Knight is a lot of hard work, but it's fulfilling," she answered with a smile.

"Well, good for you," Erica said, sharing a look with Keara.

Julissa heard the shade in the woman's tone. It reminded her that she was out of practice dealing with the undercurrents of society conversations. There was a rhythm and balance to the shade. Julissa could read with the best of them, but she had better things on her mind. Julissa looked at Amber. Her friend rolled her eyes and texted on her phone. A second later, Julissa's rang.

Amber: *Why did we invite these hoes again?*

Julissa coughed to cover her laugh. She didn't have a definitive answer to that. They'd all been together since school, and technically Keara was the one who organized the brunch. But Amber was right. They should've done this on their own. The table was full, the eight 'friends' all ready to get reacquainted since some of them were finally back in town after college. She'd been halfway dreading it, but only because she'd wanted to sleep in. Some of the ladies she was happy to reconnect with.

Julissa: *Behave.*

She shuddered. That reminded her of Rocco on Friday night. She picked up her phone and sighed. No text yet from Rocco. He said he was going over to his family's house today. She assumed that meant the Knights since she knew that Rocco had grown up in the group home Adina Knight's family ran. She'd been able to extract that tiny bit of information out of him when they talked on the phone yesterday.

"Are you going to be on your phone all lunch?" Keara asked.

"You must be waiting on a call from someone," one of her friends teased.

"A man, even." Another one said.

Keara narrowed her eyes. "You're with some-one?"

"I met my mate," she admitted, happy to finally get that out, though there was a little trepidation.

Was Rocco going around claiming her? According to her brothers, he was. She'd cursed them out yesterday about once again interfering with her life.

"Oh my God, who?"

"So it's true? Rocco Jamison is your mate?" Erica asked.

Of course, she knew. The sow had been trying to trap Julissa's brother Liam for years. Ain't no telling how much of her business her brother spilled. Some of her friends frowned.

"Silas Knight's guard?" Keara asked, snickering in disbelief.

Julissa was never one to lose her temper, and not much shook her confidence; she had her mother to thank for that. Because of that, she ignored the scorn in Keara's words, instead sharing a knowing look with Amber. Keara was a joke, her jealousy well known and ignored amongst them. Her best friend rolled her eyes. Julissa had already confided in Amber on Saturday night. The two had talked extensively about how Julissa could push her mate along.

"Have you seen that man? Good for you, Julissa. I, for one, am glad they brought new blood to the Motsi." Amber said.

"Here, here," they cheered, and Julissa snickered.

She knew that some of the crowd she hung

with were snooty, but she would not allow that to get in between her and her mate.

Despite her initial misgivings, she enjoyed brunch. She'd had one too many of the bottomless mimosas, so she caught a ride back with her security. She was stopped in the lobby of her building by the concierge. The woman handed her a floral arrangement that made her gasp. It was beautiful, the buds fragrant, and it would fit perfectly on her dining room table. She ripped open the envelope and couldn't contain the smile that covered her face.

I can't wait until you're mine.

She bit her bottom lip and debated heading to his apartment in a trench coat and nothing else. Would that be enough to push him into giving her the dick? Knowing him, he'd tell her no since she was drunk.

Boooo.

She snort-laughed at the silliness of her thoughts and reached for the second padded envelope. She opened it and smiled at all the gift cards. They were for various restaurants around the area that delivered to her building. Rocco had said he wanted to both feed and spoil her. Her heart thudded against her chest. She'd been worried that her rambling when they talked would be off-putting to him; meanwhile, he'd been listening. The restaurant gift cards were proof of that. She didn't like to cook, and his gesture ensured she would still eat.

She pulled out her phone as she stepped into the elevator, tucking the phone between her ear and shoulder as she clutched the flowers to her stomach. He answered quickly.

"Thank you, Rocco."

"You're welcome, Liss."

She didn't know what else to say. "I just wanted to hear your voice."

He growled, and her hands trembled.

"Will you be with your family all day?"

"Just about," he said.

"Text me when you get home safe," she said softly, giving him the same words he'd given her on Friday night.

He chuckled darkly. "Will do, sug."

She ended the call, smiling from ear to ear. *My mate, my mate.*

Rocco smiled down at his phone. Julissa was incredibly sweet, and he loved that. She had grown up spoiled; anyone who interacted with her for more than a second would know that, but keeping her in that lifestyle would give him great pleasure. He wasn't hurting for money, but he had worried that she would see him only as a bodyguard and nothing more. It didn't seem like she cared one way or the other. He liked that.

Iris had always told them that 'spoiled' never meant one specific thing. He'd quickly discovered that Julissa was a foodie, so he would cater to that. It seemed to be working because, from Silas' office, he could observe her soft smile and giddiness when the lunch he ordered for her every day hit her desk. Rock had scoured the web for the top restaurants in the area, checking reviews to ascertain if she would like them. He took note of her favorites, and the gift cards he'd sent over today were from those places.

Tucking his phone away, he entered the Knight's residence, his spirit light. The home of Dallas and Adina was large but still inviting. He could smell the food Iris was making for their

Sunday dinner and hear the chatter from his family as he went further into the house.

His family.

It had taken him years to get used to that. But the Knights had been patient with him. His godson whined the minute he rounded the corner into the large kitchen. Mila sat around the enormous marble island in the middle while Iris stood at the six-burner range, laughing with Adina.

Mila sucked her teeth. "I feed you. Why are you betraying me for your uncle?" She asked her son as his hand reached for him.

Rocco laughed and lifted Carter high, enjoying his happy squeal. He pulled the baby into his chest and chuckled as his godson immediately reached for his tattoos. They fascinated the baby. He greeted Adina, nuzzling her cheek and doing the same to Iris.

"Tell me about Julissa," Adina ordered straight away.

"Mama Di," he sighed. "I'm barely in the door."

She looked behind him. "Alone too. You should've brought her."

He winced as all three women turned their attention to him, tuning in. "She had plans."

"Dallas and Micah had a very animated conversation about it the other night," Adina said, waggling her eyebrows.

He chuckled at the meddling woman. "She's my mate."

Mila laughed. "Slow down, Rocco. You're giving us too much information."

The women busted out laughing. "Leave my baby alone," Adina teased.

Iris sighed. "We'll never get grandkids out of him, Adina."

He laughed at their dramatics. Mason entered the kitchen with Cici on his heels and Antonio on her hip.

"Perfect timing," he breathed, causing them to laugh again.

"Carter, my man," Mason greeted his nephew and reached for him.

Carter whined and curled tighter into Rock.

"Do you see what I'm saying about this traitor," Mila told Mason.

"Nephew, that's how you do me?" Mason grabbed the baby, loudly kissing his cheeks until he stopped whining.

Now that Rocco's arms were free, Antonio

started babbling and damn near jumped out of his mother's arms, reaching for him. Rock grabbed him, growling at his nephew, who laughed and grabbed his cheeks.

"I already know y'all are going to make my baby rough," Celine fussed, smiling.

Dallas came into the kitchen and waved for him. The male's power was potent, filling the space and making Rocco's animal alert. Despite how long Dallas Knight had been in high society, that feral energy still accompanied him. The strength of the man's panther should've made a young Rocco wary, but it had given him a sense of security that still carried over into adulthood.

He tried to give Toni back to his mama, but the kiddo gripped his shirt tightly.

"Okay then, nephew. Let's go talk business with Poppa." He'd long ago stopped worrying about how his voice sounded with the Knight children. Neither of them seemed to mind his rough timbre.

"Dinner in fifteen," Adina called after them.

"We won't take that long, love," Dallas assured her.

Rocco had been in Dallas' office many times before. The whole room fit the man to a tee. The dark green walls contrasted the oak bookshelves that held more awards than books. An entire unit housed his humidor and liquor, situated in the corner of the room behind a deep leather chair where Dallas spent much of his time. To this day, the smell of cigars and leather reminded Rocco of the man. He spotted the plants Adina had snuck into the place to 'give it more life.'

He settled into the leather chair in front of Dallas' heavy desk, sitting Antonio on his lap. Dallas slid into the one behind his desk, passing a stack of papers to Rocco.

"We're still working out details, but your mating contract is nearly done."

That surprised him. The contracts were reserved for higher-ranking families. That Dallas had required it for him proclaimed him a part of the Knight family.

Rocco frowned down at the list of his assets. "You're negotiating with Councilman Crespo?"

"Why wouldn't I? You're a member of my family." Dallas sucked his teeth. "You got me fucked up if you think I'm finna let them hose you in a contract."

His heart thundered. "PD."

Dallas held up his hand. "I just need you to mark out the hard 'no's, and I will handle the rest. I'm proud of the way you've grown the assets I gifted you with. I took great pleasure in rubbing Micah's face in the fact that my son is bringing more to the table than he thought."

Rocco couldn't help the smile that tilted his lips. "You been giving him hell?"

"You already know how I operate."

He leaned down and studied the outline of his assets, marveling how far he'd come from the boy thrown in the group home when his mother had been murdered. He owed Dallas more than the money he'd invested in him. He owed the man his life. He marked out what he wouldn't part with and passed the papers back to Dallas.

Dallas frowned at the single line. "That's it."

"It's just money, and she's my mate. I trust you." It felt good to say and mean.

Dallas' eyes softened, and he cleared his throat. "I got you. Always, I promised you that."

He nodded and stood. "Thank you. For this…for everything you've ever done for me."

The two men stared at each other, all the things

unsaid showing in their eyes. Dallas nodded, understanding all that Rocco couldn't articulate.

Eight

"Let's talk sanctuary cities," Silas announced Monday morning.

They were all gathered in chairs scattered across his office. Their office's current project was drafting a bill to protect the last sanctuary cities across this country. There were twenty left, and they were all under threat because an energy company wanted land rights for just one.

The cities had been established to protect smaller shifter packs and their rarer animals. After the war with humans, laws were put into place to leave the cities as they were, shifters only under their own individual rule. The new law would rip that independence from them. Julissa spent the first two months in her new job researching the town charters and coming up with possible solutions to close up any exploitable loopholes.

She worked to keep her eyes off her mate and focus on the meeting, but that was near impossible. She made a note to herself to find out Rock's thoughts on public displays of affection. She didn't want to cross over any of his boundaries. Julissa had been keeping her hands to herself all day, but she wondered how he would feel about that if they weren't at work. He was sitting on the sofa in Silas's office. His gaze concentrated on the laptop in front of him. She wanted to know what he was doing, but Silas' following words snagged her attention.

"Congressman Stuart is halfway to the support he needs for his new bill dismantling the Sanctuary cities in this country. That means we need to work on our counter proposal fast. But we don't want to move too fast where we leave out their needs and wants. To that end, I need a volunteer."

Julissa's arm shot up quickly. "I'll do it."

Silas sat back and narrowed his eyes. "You haven't even heard what I needed."

She adjusted in her seat and straightened. "Well, if we're drafting laws that further protect sanctuary cities, then we'll need to make sure it covers their needs and any benefits Congressman Stuart promised them to sway their vote. That means talking to the city council members and getting it directly from their mouths. I can do that. I've been studying the town charters for two months now."

Silas nodded for her to keep going.

Julissa licked her lips in nervousness. All eyes were on her, and while she was used to it, it still unnerved her. But she pushed past it. She wanted to do a great job and, most of all, for people to see her differently than just her daddy's princess.

"I'm new, I get that, but I've been in politics my whole life, and I don't mean that as hyperbole. I've shadowed my father for as long as I can remember, attending tri-council meetings and sitting in on his meetings with the bears of the city. I know how to determine the needs of the shifters we serve."

Despite her age, she had some experience parsing needs from the requests of the shifters her father ruled. Micah had never had an issue breaking down what he did to his only daughter. He may have wanted to keep her celibate her whole life, but he took pride in crafting her mind. Micah had been ecstatic about her decision to go to law school.

Silas studied her, tapping his pencil against his desk. "It's not just talking on the phone with them. You'll need to visit each city. We can set up meetings with their individual city councils from here and coordinate with the mayors. That's twenty cities in less than a month. Can you handle that?"

She nodded eagerly, fighting to keep still in her chair because, besides Silas's stare, she could now feel Rocco's prodding gaze. Julissa stood firm in her argument and swallowed down the need to fill in the silence straining the room.

"Let's get the meetings scheduled and all the information on the town charters that we can find so we can arm Julissa with the most up-to-date information," Silas ordered. "Everyone else is dismissed."

She expected jealous glances or even resentment, but the four other team members sent her thumbs up on their way to do their assigned jobs. She wanted to slouch in relief but would wait until she left Silas's office to celebrate.

Silas spoke the moment the door closed behind the last person. "It's too dangerous, Julissa."

She opened her mouth to protest, but he held up his hand.

"I understand having to prove yourself, in any case. So, I'll send you, but Rock will go with you as protection."

A thrill went through her, and she tucked her lips to hide her smile. "You think that's necessary?"

Julissa didn't look in Rocco's direction. She'd fold if she did.

"Very much so. Keisha will book all your travel arrangements. Most of the cities are concentrated in the center of the country, so it shouldn't be too taxing. Go home and pack."

"Oh…now?"

"The sooner you bring back the assessments, the sooner we can get the jump on the senator."

She nodded, but indecision froze her. Had she bitten off more than she could chew? "I…"

"Now, Julissa," Silas chided her gently, waving towards the door.

"Ok. Thank you. I won't let you down," she said, quickly getting out of her seat.

She rushed from his office, celebration forgotten. There would be no time for that.

Rocco watched her leave, his bear rumbling in his chest in anticipation. A road trip with his mate would break his resolve to keep his hands off her. That was a given. He was okay with that. It was the danger to her that he didn't like. But he would never stop her from doing the job she obviously loved. The hours she'd put in the past two months had proven that. Julissa rarely left the office before Silas did.

"You good with that?" Silas asked him.

His bear protested because even if his naive mate didn't understand the danger she was putting herself in, they did.

"Micah?"

"Pop already dealing with him for you. You just keep her alive. But also, quit pussyfooting around and mate that girl. Y'all got the whole office full of pheromones."

Rock growled, and Silas laughed. "Don't get mad at me. I already called Theo, so you're good to go home and pack. And heads up, Mom's looking for you."

He frowned and gave his best friend his full attention.

"Your niece let slip last night that your apartment 'was naked,' Ya-Ya's words, not mine."

Rock sighed. He'd let Riyah ride with him yesterday to pick up something from home, and she'd been on his ass the whole ride back to the Knight's. That little girl was determined to drag him out of his self-imposed isolation whether he liked it or not. He groaned when his phone rang, punctuating Silas' point. The only other people who called him were in this office, so he already knew who it was.

"Mama Di," he greeted.

"I didn't want to invade your privacy by entering your den. Come let Sariyah and me in," she gently ordered. "We'll meet you there."

He groaned, and she laughed. "It'll be painless," she promised.

He looked at Silas, who laughed.

"That's what you get for spoiling her," Silas said, shaking his head and returning to his paperwork.

The 'her' could've been either one of the ladies. Yes, he spoiled his niece, but he could admit he treated Adina and Iris the same. Either of the women knew that they only had to call, and he would drop what he was doing for them. Luckily for him, they didn't take advantage of that. It was one of the things he loved about them both.

"I'm on the way," he said.

She ended the call, and he lowered his head. A naked apartment. He had to chuckle. He could only imagine how the eight-year-old had described it. His mind went to Julissa; decorating his apartment would be good. He wondered what she would like and what her tastes were. He hadn't yet visited her apartment to see. He'd be out of town for who knew how long, so in reality, he didn't have to go through every step of the redecorating process.

That was tolerable.

He headed to his apartment to pack and deal with his niece and her grandmother. They were there when he pulled up to his building. Sariyah quickly jumped from Adina's Bentley, rushing towards him. Her kinky hair was spilling from the bottom of the pink beret she wore that matched her sweater and boots. Her brown skin was flushed with excitement.

"Uncle Rock, we're going to get stuff for your house," she said excitedly. "Aren't you excited?"

He grunted his answer to that. "My place is fine," he said gruffly.

She smiled at him, her missing teeth making her extra adorable. "Sure, sure."

She grabbed his hand and dragged him towards Adina. The Knight matriarch was dressed identically to her granddaughter, except her grey and black hair was straight and flowing around her shoulders. She was a beautiful woman. Graceful and powerful, the energy from her panther was always at the forefront. Adina carried her panther well and had never tried to conform with the humans.

"Mama Di."

Adina smiled and cupped his cheek. Her power soothed him. "You know I would leave it be, but your niece is insistent."

"I'll be gone."

Adina's face creased with worry. "With Silas?"

He nodded to their security. "Inside."

She hummed in understanding, and they all marched towards the secured building. He greeted the doorman and headed to the elevator. Ya-Ya prattled on with her grandmother as they rode up. Sariyah stepped off the elevator, but she didn't approach his door. He smiled. The little girl learned fast. They didn't play about keeping Sariyah safe. Before opening his door, he checked to ensure his security measures were still in place. He swept the area, using his senses before giving them the all-clear.

He sighed, knowing what would happen the moment Adina realized how he was living. It wasn't that he couldn't afford better. It was just that growing up the way he had, nothing was permanent, least of all a home, so he planned accordingly. He kept his prized possessions in his bedroom, hidden in his closet. Outside of the bedroom furniture and sofa, there was nothing else in the apartment.

Adina narrowed her eyes at him before dropping her purse on the small kitchen counter. She took out her phone and started taking notes. He thought about how Julissa would feel knowing he'd been in the building for nearly a decade. He hadn't corrected her on Friday night when she'd rightfully assumed he'd just moved in. The place was sparse, and it was the first time he'd been embarrassed by that. He didn't allow people into his house, so he'd never had to worry about it before.

Knowing there was nothing he could do, he headed to his room to pack. He was nearly done but tensed when he felt Adina's presence.

"How long will you be gone?"

He shrugged.

"Alone?"

"With Julissa."

Adina's eyes widened in happiness.

"Protection." He warned her.

"Sure, sure. I talked to Therese. Dallas and Micah have nearly finished negotiating the mating contract, but it's handled."

He nodded again.

"Be careful, my love."

"I will," he promised, zipping his wardrobe bag and small suitcase.

She waited until he left the walk-in closet to hug him. Adina understood that being in an enclosed space with him could set him off. He loved that about her. She read him like no other person. She held him tight, her panther sending out soothing energy.

"Call me when you get where you're going and if you need anything."

He inclined his head towards the living room.

She sighed. "If I didn't understand why, I would be so mad at you, Rocco. It's okay to settle in. You own the building. No one can take this place from you."

He grunted.

"I'm moving you to the penthouse where you belong. You have the whole fourth floor you could be in."

He raised an eyebrow.

Adina chuckled. "That's not the same. I am not taking away your home. I'm attempting to nudge you into making one for yourself and your soon-to-be mate."

He didn't bother arguing, but she seemed to sense his reluctance.

"You're never going to allow more than three or four tenants in this dang gone building, so don't act like you'll have an influx of renters vying for that condo. I'll make sure that the place is aired out so that no extra scents linger when the movers finish."

He nuzzled her cheek and grabbed his suitcase.

"I'll keep your mate in mind too." She said to his back.

He stopped walking and debated turning. Adina

wiped away the smug smile as he gave in and turned around.

"I'll ask Therese for her likes and dislikes...discreetly, of course." He stared, and she laughed. "I can be discreet, Rocco Jamison. You'll bring her by the house for dinner when you're back."

Adina held up her hands when he said nothing to that. "She's beautiful. I won't rush you, but I can't speak for Iris."

He grunted in amusement.

She walked closer to him and cupped his cheek. "You understand that your parent's mating has no bearing on what you'll have with Julissa?"

"Ma," he said softly.

"I know you fear that you'll be like him. I took over raising you when your mother could no longer. I don't raise cowards, and I for damn sure don't raise men who put their hands on women. You're nothing like him." She insisted, her animal's power filling him.

He nuzzled into her hand, his throat tight. Adina had always been able to read him and his fears. Despite her words, apprehension about the mating trapped him. He kept that to himself.

"Go, be careful, and keep in touch." She said softly, letting him off the hook.

He nodded and headed out. Sariyah was waiting for him when he reached his living room. Instead of making notes, she watched his TV and ate the fruit from his refrigerator. It seemed her grandmother would be doing all the redecorating herself. He chuckled.

She jumped up when she saw him. "Bye, Uncle Rock. Be careful on your trip. Bring me back something."

"Just something?" he asked.

Sariyah gave him a sly look. He smiled and lifted her, nuzzling her cheek. The little minx. Her tight hug soothed the anxiety brought on by her grandmother's words. She wrapped her arms around his neck, the charms on her bracelet jingling. He bought her one from every city he and her dad visited.

"Be good for your parents." He finally said.

"You know me," she said instead, and he huffed out a small laugh.

He loved the busybody and was happy his friend had found her and his mate. Rocco checked his email as he rode down the elevator. Keisha had already sent over the itinerary. He raised his eyebrows at how much driving they would be doing but pushed it aside. His only priority would be keeping Julissa safe.

Nine

Rock drove his personal car, parking his vintage Lincoln Continental into the spot reserved for the passengers of private jets. Silas would pick it up on his way home this evening, so he didn't have to worry about it while he was gone. He didn't like the idea of anyone driving his baby, but Silas would be careful. Julissa was already on the tarmac waiting when he walked up. A bear was beside her, his all-black uniform and alert demeanor screaming security. His mate had changed out of her work suit and wore a skin-tight black jumpsuit and a camel-colored trench coat on top. The coat did nothing to hide the curves underneath, and Rock's mouth watered, his bear rising enough to push out his claws. He took a deep calming breath before approaching her.

"My father insisted on a guard," she grumbled as he walked up. "Never mind that I'm trying to do my job. I don't need two of you."

He grunted at her tone, and she sighed.

"I'm not trying to sound ungrateful."

He held out his hand, and the other bear shook. "Byron. I've heard a lot about you around town. You'll have point, but Councilman Crespo thought another pair of hands couldn't hurt."

He nodded because the more eyes on his mate, the better. She was fussing about him and Byron, but another guard was already on the plane. Julian had sent him ahead like he did anytime Silas and Rock traveled. He inclined his head towards the private plane, and the bear got the hint, moving quickly towards the jet with Julissa's luggage. She had packed for a solid month, it seemed.

Rocco's gaze never left Julissa, cataloging her irritation. He lifted her chin. It wasn't his first touch with his mate, and still, his hands shook. She was pouting, and damn if it didn't do things to his bear.

"Will we have a problem with the extra security?"

She shook her head and dropped her gaze. She

shuddered, and he wondered if the timbre of his voice was too much for her. No fear laced her divine scent, so that was a no.

"Itinerary?"

She nodded. "Keisha sent it and all the other details we need for the first town."

He didn't move, simply soaking her in. He lost his fight with temptation and skimmed his hands down her waist, bringing her into his body. She sighed and relaxed in his embrace.

"You ready?"

She nodded and put her forehead into his chest. "I'm looking forward to alone time with you."

"Won't be alone." He reminded her.

She sucked her teeth, which made him chuckle. She joined him, sliding her arms into his jacket and around his waist.

"What you want, sug?"

"You," she whispered, and he shuddered, tightening his fingers on her waist.

"I'm yours, Liss."

She looked up, surprise coloring her face. He threw caution to the wind and kissed her. He needed it like his next breath. Julissa melted into the kiss, her bear reaching out to his. The two animals sent out magic, brushing against each other, and Rock was ready to drag her back to his car. He pulled back and groaned.

"Daddy says our contract is done," she said softly.

He growled as his phone rang. He whipped it from his pocket.

"Yeah, PD."

"Contract done," Dallas announced, confirming her words.

He stared down at his mate, his bear bucking because nothing was stopping him from claiming Julissa. All of a sudden, the trip looked better and better. Julissa nuzzled into him, her hands making slow circles on his back in a soothing motion.

"Bet."

"How long y'all gon' be gone?"

"Not sure. A few weeks."

"Be careful. Julian sent extra guards?" Dallas asked.

"He did."

"Ok. Then keep us posted. Love you, kid."

"You too." He ended the call, thinking about everything he could do to his mate when he got her alone.

"Let's go, sug," he ordered.

He escorted her onto the plane. His eyes raked the interior, and he got the all-okay signal from the guards already posted in their seats towards the back. That left him and Julissa in the front alone. The jet was big enough to hold Silas's entire staff, so there was enough space between Rocco and Julissa that they would have a small semblance of privacy. He settled her into a chair before taking the one next to her. Julissa tensed as the flight attendant went through her checks. Her leg started bouncing, and her bear's energy was erratic. He placed a hand on her knee to still it.

"What's wrong?"

"Nervous flyer," she admitted. "Talk to me to distract me."

He snorted, and she laughed, knowing how that request would go. But he could think of another way to distract her.

JULISSA KNEW ASKING Rocco to talk to her as a distraction was a ridiculous ask. The man only spoke when necessary. She turned in her seat to face him.

"Why do you call Councilman Knight 'PD'?"

He stared at her for a moment, and she didn't think he would answer.

"Buckle, sug." He ordered as the flight attendant signaled they would take off soon.

She did what he ordered, still waiting on his answer. She gripped the sides of the chair as the plane taxied. He pulled her hand into his lap.

"Papa D. I shortened it to just PD after a while. It stuck." His gravelly voice calmed her fear, and she gripped his hand tightly.

The small plane was bumping across the runway, and she was working on regulating her breathing. Her nerves had her animal frazzled. Rock leaned over and nuzzled into her neck, huffing against her skin. She froze in shock and pleasure, her nervousness momentarily forgotten.

"Smell good," he rumbled.

She tilted her head to give him more space, and he scraped his teeth against her skin, sucking on her neck. She swallowed and squirmed in her seat as moisture gathered at the apex of her thighs. His hand traced her thighs, and her breath shorted in anticipation.

"What are you doing?" she whispered.

She cursed her idea to wear the full bodysuit.

She would give anything to be in a skirt right now. Rocco tilted her chin towards him and kissed her gently, licking her bottom lip.

"Distracting you," was his answer.

He kissed her again, and she opened her mouth, and he slid his tongue inside. She lost herself in the kiss, her body flushing in pleasure. He couldn't get inside her pants, but it didn't stop him from pressing his thumb against her pussy, expertly finding her clit. *Fuck*, she was going to come all over herself. He didn't move his finger; instead, he exerted just enough pressure that her stomach clenched.

"Is it working?"

She rocked her hips forward and nodded. Oh, it was definitely fucking working. He pinched her nipple, and Julissa sucked in a sharp breath. She couldn't help the whimper that escaped. She bit down on her lip to keep herself from moaning.

"Nah, let me hear that shit. Tell me how good I'm making you feel."

The rumble of his voice raised the hair on the back of her neck. Her stomach dipped as the plane took off. He pressed a little harder against her clit, and Julissa moved her hips in a circle to ride that feeling.

"Rocco," she whispered, mindful that there were not alone on this plane.

"Feel good, mama?"

"Yes," she hissed as he circled her nipple slowly.

She reached down and held his hand in place, writhing her hips. She could feel an orgasm on the horizon.

"Breathe, baby," he whispered, nipping her ear lobe.

She let out a shuddering breath. "So close."

He nuzzled his cheek against her neck, the hair of his beard scraping against her skin. The added sensation sent electricity tingling across her skin. Her body tightened, and Rock lifted his head. He gripped her chin and turned her to face him. His gaze was dark...hungry. His animal stared from his eyes, a feral look that made her pussy clench in need.

"I want to see your face when you come." He kissed her softly. "I'm gon' memorize that shit."

Julissa closed her eyes, but he nipped her chin hard, the pain spiking her pleasure. It forced her lids open, and she could only stare at him in helpless wonder as her body went up in flames. Rocco kissed her hard, his tongue spearing her mouth as she rode out her orgasm.

He pulled back. "Claws, baby." He whispered against her lips.

She looked down and noticed the scratches on his arm. "Oh my God, I'm so sorry, Rocco."

She hadn't even been aware her animal was that close to the surface. Her cheeks flamed in embarrassment. There was no pain on his face, just satisfaction as he chuckled and inspected his arm.

"I'll never stop you from marking your shit, sug." He hovered over her mouth, not kissing her, just inhaling. "You smell amazing. I can't wait to have you in my mouth."

Julissa squeezed her thighs together at that thought. For a man who said few words, he definitely knew the right ones to use. She took a deep breath as her body calmed. She was utterly relaxed and euphoric. She lifted his arm and snuggled into his chest. His heartbeat was steady, and the sound soothed her like nothing she'd ever experienced.

He curled his arm around her waist and kissed the top of her head. "Try to sleep. We got a long night ahead."

She hummed in answer, already halfway there.

Ten

Julissa had been happy for the nap that she'd been able to snag on the plane. Seven hours of traveling was no joke. It was well into the evening when they'd arrived at the small Montana airport, and it was colder than a bitch outside too. She let her bear off its leash to warm her as she waited for the SUV they'd rented to drive up. It didn't take long, but she had felt every second of the wait. Rocco escorted her into the running truck and helped the others get the bags inside. She looked down at the reservations Keisha sent over.

"There weren't any hotels in town, just a bed and breakfast." She informed Rocco as he got inside with her.

"What does that mean?" He gruffly asked.

"There were only two rooms. The two of them

should share the larger one, which leaves the one with only one bed for us." She fought not to smile at Rocco's hungry look.

The guards in front of her snickered.

"It's just two nights; we'll survive." She teased them.

Rocco simply grunted and tapped Byron on the shoulder to get him to move along. The bear was driving while Harold took the passenger seat. They had another hour in the car before they reached their destination. The sanctuary towns were small and, luckily, clustered not too far from each other. After this town, instead of another flight, they just had a four-hour drive to the next one. She would see more Middle America than she wanted but was over-excited about her task.

Julissa gasped an hour later when they pulled up to the white-washed building that was their bed and breakfast. She saw small glimpses of cottages towards the back that were all white and adobe style, the stone beautifully kept. It was quaint and beautiful. She didn't know what she was expecting, but this romantic place had not been it. She wanted to squeal in pleasure.

She waited until Rocco let her out of the car,

but she gripped his hand, rushing inside to see the rest of the place. The stone floors were meticulously maintained, and she could smell the wood burning from the giant fireplace that was the focal point in the room. Leather chairs and sofas were scattered across the room, with colorful pillows covering them. A few guests were having drinks, but the place was empty otherwise.

The owner struck up a conversation with Rocco while he checked them in or, well, attempted to. He gave her a polite smile and filled out the required paperwork, sliding the woman his credit card. Julissa shrugged when the woman looked at her.

"Is there a place that serves dinner here?"

"We have a diner that's still open for a couple of more hours," she answered with a smile, handing Rocco their keys. "The only other foxes in town run it. Just tell them you're staying here, and they'll send the tab here if you want."

Julissa nodded. "Thank you so much."

She was anxious to see their room first. Rocco handed off the keys to Harold and Byron, gripping Julissa's hand as they walked out the back door of the main building. She gasped. Lights were strung across the desert setting, and despite the snow that covered everything, it looked magical. Rocco walked her to their small cabin, and she was happy to be out of the cold. The queen-sized bed was inviting. There was a small bathroom off to their left, but a bathtub sat directly in front of the bed and the wall-to-wall window that looked out towards the snowy landscape. It was breathtaking.

"I can sleep on the sofa for tonight. You need to concentrate on the meetings ahead," Rocco's voice rumbled.

She sucked her teeth. "I can control myself if you sleep beside me, Rocco."

Maybe.

She'd see, wouldn't she?

THE ANSWER WAS YES, she could control herself, but she was grumpy as hell and horny to boot. Not a good way to start her first meeting of the trip, but there was nothing to be done about it. She looked out into the gathering crowd of the school gym that doubled as their town hall, her stomach fluttering with nervousness. Rocco stood at her back while Byron and Harold were scattered throughout the crowd at the exit points.

She politely waited her turn as the town alpha and mayor introduced her and her purpose for visiting. There were murmurs and questions scoffing at her age, but she ignored them, focusing on the speech Silas had sent ahead. Taking a deep breath, she took the podium.

The speech took twenty minutes, which wasn't long enough to cover all the ways their new bill would help, but it gave the bullet points. The mayor and his council would get the full breakdown tomorrow. For now, it was more about opening the floor up for inquiries. Her eyes widened when she realized how many people had questions when she was done.

"Why does this Knight want to help us all of a sudden?" One of the townspeople asked.

She took a deep breath and considered her answer. "Mr. Knight just wants to ensure he's representing your true needs and wants without you giving up any of your independence. It's not all of a sudden. His position as Liaison to this county's shifters requires that he certifies we're all represented."

"Councilman Stuart promised more money coming into this town."

She nodded. "I'm sure that's true. But he doesn't tell you that federal money comes at a cost. Your independence is its first toll. You'll have to answer and account for every penny the government gives to this town. And again, I'm not here to talk you out of voting. If that's what you want, then Mr. Knight can add you as an exception to our bill. You'll get the federal money, and your town will be disbanded. What our bill does is stop the blanket dismantling of sanctuary cities. It may not mean anything to your town, but there are smaller towns still counting on the protections sanctuary status provides for them."

The murmuring from the crowd picked up at her words.

"How do we know he's not feeding us false information?"

She smiled. It was a fair question. "Mr. Knight's website lists all the bills he's passed and how they've assisted this country's shifters. There are resources there for you to research for yourself. You don't have to take my word on anything."

That seemed to pacify the crowd, and they

settled. Julissa stepped back from the podium and allowed their alpha to take control.

ROCCO'S GAZE SPLIT TIME between his mate and the restless crowd. There were a couple of specific males he was keeping his eyes on. They didn't look interested in the proceedings; instead, their gaze was on Julissa. He could understand that, though. It was fascinating watching her speak. He'd seen how she controlled a room when he attended Motsi events; this town hall was no different. She was confident in her manner and charming in her words. He watched her settle the fears of the townspeople without losing her temper. Empathy and compassion coated her every word, and though many of the shifters had given her a hard time, she seemed to be winning over some of them. It was a huge turn-on.

Though, it seemed everything she did was a turn-on for him. The alpha dismissed the meeting, and some people swarmed toward Julissa to ask more questions.

He stepped in front of her, "Two feet." he ordered them, and they stopped and formed a line.

He dodged questions some of the women in town aimed his way, keeping vigilant at Julissa's side. His mate was damn near growling by the time another female walked up to him. Her bear became agitated and more aggravated as the questions kept coming, so he cut it all short.

"Time to go," he ordered her.

She sighed in relief and smiled. "Thank you all for your questions. I'll make sure Mr. Knight understands all of your concerns."

He guided her to the SUV and helped her inside. The heels she wore were not necessarily practical for snow. Instead of closing the door, he turned her legs so that they buffered his waist. He leaned over into her space. She sucked in a sharp breath, her bear reaching for his as she wrapped her arms around his shoulders. He allowed his animal off the leash to soothe her.

"You got a jealous streak," he said softly.

She sighed. "How would you like it if males were all over me?"

He chuckled, "That tells me you ain't paying no attention to your surroundings, sug."

The men in town had been eyeing her from the moment she walked her fine ass into that school gymnasium. The yellow suit she wore beneath the trench accentuated her every curve and made her stand out like a ray of sunshine. He hadn't been the only one to notice.

He lifted her chin. "What do you need from me?"

Her pulse raced beneath his thumb as he gripped her neck loosely.

"I...what do you mean?"

"I got this thing with jealousy. It sets off my bear and not in a good way. Tell me why you worried about other women."

Though her jealousy didn't feel toxic, it, unfortunately, triggered way too many memories, and he wanted to nip it in the bud asap. She searched his eyes, debating what to tell him.

"You haven't tried to claim me even though our contracts are finished. It makes my bear insecure." She whispered.

"I'm moving too slow for her?" He nuzzled into her neck, and the animal in her flared and wrapped around him.

She nodded in response.

"I'm sorry, love. I...got a few hang-ups. I don't know if you should tie yourself to someone like me."

She growled. "Don't talk about my mate like that."

He smiled, a slight tilt of his lips. He kissed Julissa gently before pulling away. "Buckle, sug."

He closed the door carefully and walked around the truck. He needed to sit with what she was telling him. He didn't want to acerbate her insecurity, but he was having difficulty with his own where she was concerned. He had better examples of matings that worked, so he knew they wouldn't all end like his parents' had. But he was still wary.

"Do you have any idea what you want for lunch, Liss?" he asked to break the silence.

She groaned. "I don't even want to think about it. I want a nap."

He chuckled, knowing the work she still had to do before she could relax. "I'll take care of it."

She gave him a smile that warmed his whole body. "Thank you, Rocco."

He loved the way she said his name. He gripped her chin and brought her closer, kissing her firmly. He pulled back when they pulled into the driveway of the bed and breakfast. The woman made him lose his head.

Eleven

Lunch was a thing of the past, and by the darkening skies, it was time for dinner. Julissa happily ended the Zoom call with her coworkers, happy to be done for the day. They'd reviewed the townspeople's concerns and devised a strategy for tomorrow's meeting with the mayor. Rocco had long ago left her alone in the room. She stood, stretched, and debated whether or not she should shower before hunting down her mate and something for dinner. Instead of doing either, she checked in with her parents.

Her mother had been sending her messages and pictures all day. She went through them now that she had time and shook her head. Why was Therese sending her furniture pictures? She dialed her mother.

"Lady, you better not be trying to redecorate my place," was how she greeted her mother.

Therese laughed. "Girl. I just wanted your opinion. My life does not revolve around you."

"Since when?" Julissa joked.

"Which one of the sofas did you like?" Therese prodded.

"Mama, I don't even know where you're putting it. How am I supposed to answer that?" She unbuttoned her pants and slipped out of the tight trousers, sighing in relief.

"Pick, Julissa. Why are you so argumentative?" Her mother grumbled.

Julissa snorted in amusement. "Fine. You know I love velvet, so the green one."

"Now, was that so hard?" Therese asked.

"What are you up to?"

Julissa put the phone on speaker and changed into something comfortable but appropriate for dinner if Rocco decided they would go out. Though, she was hoping he wouldn't want to.

"None of your business."

Julissa laughed outright. Oh yeah, her mother was definitely up to something.

"How was your first day?" Therese changed the subject.

"It was good. I felt like they were receptive, but we won't really know until the result of the vote comes out."

She looked up as Rocco came into the room. He was carrying a load of takeout trays. The smell wafted over to her, and her stomach rumbled on cue. She inhaled and closed her eyes as the scent of barbecue filled her senses. Julissa could even smell the chocolate cake hiding somewhere in those containers. She did a little dance that caught Rocco's attention. He smiled and shook his head. He cleared the small table where she had been working all day and set it for their dinner.

"Julissa," Therese called, bringing her attention back to the conversation she'd been having with her mother.

"Sorry, Mom. What did you say?"

Therese sighed dramatically. "Never mind. Just answer my texts when I send them. In a timely fashion if you please."

"Mama, do not rearrange my apartment. I mean it. I'll get to those boxes in my own time."

"I love you. Keep me posted when you can, love." Therese quickly ended the call.

Julissa sucked her teeth and tossed her phone to the bed. Ain't no telling what that woman was doing to her apartment. She would probably have to change it all back around when she returned home. She moved closer to the table her mate was setting. Instead of just putting the food down, he'd arranged it into place settings, even going so far as to add a small flower as a centerpiece. She smiled.

God, this man.

"Where did you get these plates and stuff?" she asked, peeking at the array of food.

"Downstairs." Was all he said in that rumbly tone of his.

The man wouldn't talk, but obviously, he missed nothing. The food he'd laid out was some of her favorite barbecue choices— sausage, ribs, even down the corn and potato salad. There was no chicken on her side of the table at all. She only ate chicken when it was fried, and even that was sporadic. He'd remembered.

"You got my favorites." She said it aloud just to confirm her thoughts.

"Come," he ordered, pointing to the chair he held out.

She settled into the chair. "How did you know what to order me?"

"I listen when you talk, Liss."

"Rocco," she whispered, her cheeks heated.

She knew that was all she was getting out of him. They ate in silence. She didn't have the energy to talk, and Rocco never felt the need to fill in quiet. She thought it would make her nervous, but it didn't. Her bear was settling, and that was so puzzling to her. She didn't see a mate like Rocco for herself. She thought she would mate with someone like her father, ambitious and slick, but her bear was adamant about this indomitable man sitting across from them.

She put the first bite of chocolate cake in her mouth and moaned. Rock stilled across from her. She closed her eyes on the next taste, and when she opened them, he was staring at her, his eyes dark, dark, onyx. She stared at his bear, the feral animal watching her. She licked her lips, and he mirrored that. He sucked in a sharp breath and pulled back, his animal retreating.

He stood. "I need to..." he didn't finish the sentence.

He rushed from their room, leaving her flustered in her chair. So he wasn't entirely unaffected by her. She smiled. She could work with that.

ROCK MADE ANOTHER ROUND around the small bed and breakfast. The foxes who owned it had well-marked their territory. They were well known in the small city, so he wasn't worried about the town's residents bothering them, but he didn't slow his steps as he lumbered across the property. He'd spotted unfamiliar tracks a little too close to their cabin for his comfort, so he'd loosened the leash on his animal as he circled the property. It reminded him that he needed to stay vigilant. He couldn't have his head messed up by mating with Julissa just yet.

Satisfied that all the scents outside matched those inside, he returned to their cabin.

His bear was slamming against him to shift, but he refused to give the bear any more leeway. He already knew what the damned animal wanted, or rather who. He didn't understand how his mate could make the simple act of eating so sensual, but he had been seconds from snatching her across the table and devouring her the way she had done that cake. He was hard as stone, and it was uncomfortable at this point. Something needed to give.

The contracts were completed, and nothing stopped him from claiming Julissa...except his fear. He wasn't sure if he could be gentle with her at first. He wanted her with a ferocity that scared him. He would do anything not to hurt his mate. He let himself into their room and wished he'd insisted they find a regular hotel with separate rooms. Staying with her was going to be the death of him. He heard the shower going and *swear to God* he would break.

She came out in a robe, her face dewy from her night cream and her hair wrapped and pinned. Some of it escaped her scarf, moist and sticking to the sides of her face and temple. His feet moved. Maybe he could've stopped himself had he let his bear run off the energy, but he didn't think so. He walked to her and grabbed her into his arms. Julissa released a whoosh of air, surprise written all over her face.

He lowered his head and kissed her. A small kiss, just a little one to satisfy him and his animal. Except…Julissa went up on her toes and opened her mouth, her tongue tracing his closed mouth, asking for entrance. He obliged her—as if he could ever deny this woman. At the first taste of her, his knees went weak, and every cell in his body tuned itself to her. His bear even paused its fight with him.

She sighed, and her arms went around his waist as she kissed him deeper. Her hands trailed up and down his back, her body going soft and pliant in his arms. How could a kiss both soothe and rile him up at the same time? He lifted her and planted her on the small chest of drawers. Her legs parted, and she pulled him between them. She drew back from the kiss and buried her face between his neck and shoulder.

"Are you done fighting, my love?"

He shuddered at the longing in her voice and the feel of her breathing along his neck. Was he done? They were from two different worlds. Yeah, he moved along the periphery of hers, but still. He didn't belong, no matter that the Knights didn't seem to get that memo. She kissed his neck and clutched him tight, sighing.

"You're going to make me beg, aren't you?"

"Never, sug." He gripped her chin and brought her up for another kiss.

This time, he savored her kiss, eating at her mouth. She returned the energy, and the scent of her arousal rose between them. She gripped his dick and squeezed, and Rock pulled back.

"You're fighting me and your bear, Rocco. Put us out of our misery," she pouted, and God, his chest hurt.

She was so fucking beautiful.

"I'm not fit for you, Liss." He whispered, nuzzling against her cheek.

"Bullshit. Our animals don't make mistakes. You're mine, which means I'm made for you. Next excuse."

He studied her eyes and saw the look that he'd come to recognize. His mate was stubborn and determined. The shit that made her good at her new job was making it hard to keep his distance.

"I can't protect you if my head is fucked, Liss."

"I want my mate," she whispered.

Rock tried to swallow past the lump in his

throat. She rubbed against him, the heat from her pussy scorching him through his clothes. It made him realize that she wore nothing under that robe.

"Liss," he groaned.

"Rocco," she mocked.

He kissed her to shut her up. She grabbed his hand and brought it to her wet center, and his hands shook as he gently slid his finger across her clit. She moaned in his mouth. She pulled back and kissed down his neck, her hands going to his pants. She unbuttoned them. He should stop them. If he went past this line, there was no coming back. All the reasons he'd made up for them to wait flew out the window. He wanted her. She hummed in appreciation when she finally got his pants down his waist. His chest swelled.

He tried one more time to make her see reason. "We still have work to do. You don't want to wait until after the meeting tomorrow?"

"Fuck work." She muttered, nipping the skin of his shoulder.

Her eyes were focused as though she was already picking out a place to put her mark. He didn't know how it was possible to get harder, but his dick jumped in anticipation. Her soft hand wrapped around his erection, and every thought in his brain scattered.

"I need a shower."

She growled, her bear making its displeasure known.

He laughed at the insistent animal.

"Was that a full-on laugh?" She leaned back and smiled at him. "I might just be breaking you down, Rocco Jamison."

He snorted and lifted her, walking her to their bed. He laid her down and took his time parting the robe, opening it like a long-awaited present. He kissed her chest.

"Stay."

"I'm not going anywhere," she told him.

He smiled, and her eyes softened. He was done fighting this woman.

Twelve

Julissa took a shaky breath when she heard the shower stop. Her body was a mass of neediness, and she couldn't wait until he touched her. She wanted to know if he matched all the daydreams she'd spun about him. He came out of the bathroom with just a towel swung around his hips, and her pulse raced. He was gorgeous, his body ink-stained, mapped with muscles and dewy skin. Her mouth watered.

His eyes were on hers, intense, dark, and flashing with his animal. Her bear answered, heating Julissa's body, making her skin sensitive to the sheets she lay on.

"You moved." his voice rumbled.

She swallowed, unable to say anything. All she'd done was move up the bed to lean against the headboard. Her heartbeat thumped in her chest, her bear roiling inside. Rocco growled and closed his eyes, inhaling deeply. When he opened them, her breath caught at the molten darkness in his gaze. He looked at her as if she was the most important thing in his life.

"Rocco," she whispered.

He dragged her legs roughly, pulling until her ass was perched right on the edge of the bed. That aggressiveness should've given her pause, but her clit pulsed, and pussy quivered in yearning. His hands were tight on her thighs, but he took a shuddering breath and gentled his touch. She gasped when he went to his knees, parting her thighs and growling. Longing and lust infused the sound, and she'd never felt as wanted as he made her feel.

"In my life, I never imagined I would have anything as beautiful as you." He kissed the top of her mound, his gaze spearing her for a hot moment before his finger grazed the lips of her pussy gently. He kissed her there softly, hissing when he found her wet. "Are you mine, Julissa?"

"Yes," she rushed out.

He shuddered, his tongue sliding against her

sex. It sent shivers of desperate need down her spine.

"One last time to save yourself, sug, because once I have you, I'm not letting another soul take you from me." The intensity of his gaze brought tears to her eyes.

She ran her hand over his head, guiding him where she needed him. "You're mine, and I'll fight the world to keep you," she swore. The fire that lit his eyes warmed her from the inside. "Now, quit teasing me, Rocco."

He took that as his go signal, devouring her. With his tongue and fingers, he explored her pussy, mapping every pleasure point. His nails dug into her thighs, sometimes scraping against a spot she didn't even know was that sensitive. Every time he sucked her clit into his mouth, Julissa's back left the bed in a high arch.

"So fucking good," he murmured, his eyes on her pussy as though he'd been waiting forever to taste her.

"Rocco," she whispered his name.

He undid her, sucking, biting, and scratching until she screamed with the force of her orgasm.

He gentled his sucking until her tensed muscles loosened. He licked his lips and moaned.

"Your taste is something I'll be addicted to."

"Let me see," she whispered, gripping his arms and bringing him close.

The feral growl that rumbled his chest brought her bear forward, the wanton animal wanting her to get straight to the marking. Her claws dropped, and it spurred Rocco forward. He dropped his towel and slid up her body. She licked against his lips before kissing him. Their tongues lazily tangled, and her mind floated along a wave of bliss. Her body was limp with satiation.

Julissa found herself further under his spell. He pulled back and lifted her legs and settled them into the crook of his arms, holding her legs wide.

"Please."

"You ready, sug?" He probed the entrance of her sex with his dick, waiting on her answer.

She eagerly nodded, wanting every last bit of him. She hadn't been prepared for so much of him, though. She whimpered as he stretched her, her clenching muscles fighting against the sweet invasion.

"So tight," Rocco murmured. He nuzzled into her neck. "Let me in, sug."

His words worked, and her pussy relaxed, her stomach fluttering at the rough pleading.

"That's right, baby, relax and take me," he encouraged, his strokes leisurely and shallow until her body adjusted.

She held him tightly against her as sensations bombarded her. Feral and dominating power rushed over her as his bear pushed forward. Rocco hissed as he slid out, cursing and plunging back inside, deeper now that she'd adjusted to his size. Julissa arched her hips, taking more of him.

"This..." he paused and shook his head. "This pussy finna have me wildin', I can tell."

He released one of her legs and leaned down into her. He made love to her, his strokes gentle and deep, igniting a fire within her that threatened to burn her to ash. He was careful with her, and her bear wasn't having it. She swirled her hips and tightened down on his dick.

"More," she whispered.

He cursed. "Why you rushing me, sug? I'm trying to enjoy my pussy."

She scraped her nails down his back, allowing

her bear to fill her body. The resulting power surge sped his hips, and Rocco drove into her with fiery strokes that made her frantic. Even her dreams couldn't touch the almost desperate and carnal need between them. She screamed as he hit a spot inside that had her stomach contracting tightly.

"That's the sound I want to hear," he told her, nipping the skin of her neck.

Her bear stilled within her. His nips turned into small bites as he worked his way down to her shoulder. Julissa tilted her head, nearly begging for him to mark her and make her his. He chuckled, lifting her leg to fuck her deeper.

"Waiting on my bite, Liss?"

She whimpered. "Please, Rocco."

"Give me what I want first," he murmured, sliding his free hand between her legs to pluck at her clit.

"There," she whispered hoarsely, swiveling her hips, chasing her climax.

"Mhmm, that's a good girl; give me that nut."

He licked her shoulder and growled, the vibrations on her skin sending her over the edge. Julissa screamed, tightening down on his dick, and Rocco gave her what she wanted. His teeth pierced her shoulder, and his power flooded her body, prolonging her orgasm. His bear moved through her, twining with hers.

Rocco released her leg and cupped the back of her head. Instinct was already moving her. She sucked on the skin of his shoulder before biting down. He cursed, his hips frantically driving into her as she shoved her power into him, marking him deeply. She wanted no question as to whom he belonged. Rocco came with a yell. She pulled her teeth but continued to suck on that spot until his body shook on top of hers.

"Enough, sug," he husked out.

She acquiesced, licking the bite closed. Rocco pulled her into his body tightly, rolling until she was on top of him. He didn't pull out; he simply held her close.

"Even in my wildest dreams, Liss," he whispered against her temple.

She nuzzled into his sweaty chest, basking in their tight bond. Her bear was quiet and content. Her heart was whole, knowing she would know his emotions at any given moment. It would keep him from hiding his needs from her. She loved the thought of that.

"Gonna sleep," she said drowsily.

He kissed her forehead. "Shower or you won't be able to sleep well."

Unfortunately, that was true. "You gotta tote me."

He laughed and rolled over, lifting them off the bed. If she thought Rocco was done with her, she had been mistaken. Their shower had turned into sex, followed by more sex. By the time her mate let her rest, it was well past midnight, and Julissa didn't have a single complaint about it.

ROCCO JERKED UP, his heart racing, his breathing shallow as the nightmare played through his head. Sweat coated his skin, the uncomfortable sticky feeling a reminder of all the nights he'd laid in his childhood bed worried what the night, and hell, morning would bring. When his mother was alive, he'd feared the heavy footfalls of his father coming home drunk. After she'd died, insecurity with his various living situations had kept him up many nights. He took a deep breath and slid from the bed.

He walked into the bathroom and splashed water on his face. He scented Julissa before her arms slid around his waist.

"What's wrong?" She slid her cheek against his back, nuzzling his skin.

"Nightmare." He tensed, not wanting to admit that.

"I can feel your bear. Is it safe enough to run?"

His body relaxed when she didn't pry further. Happy to have his mind on something else, he went through his memory of the town's layout before nodding. It was a shifter-only town, so theoretically, it would be safe to shift, but that didn't mean they would be safe. His thoughts went to the tracks he hadn't recognized, but he pushed them aside. Rocco was confident he could take care of his mate.

"Let's let him out for a while. Plus, mine is anxious to meet her mate." She kissed his shoulder and walked out of the bathroom.

They threw on robes and walked out of the French doors of their room. It led to the back of the property and would have the privacy they needed to shift. Julissa dropped her robe and shifted first. He waited, giving her bear time to meet him. The sow rushed to him, butting against his chest with her head. He smiled and ran his hands through her fur. His bear pushed against his skin, impatient. Still, he took his time, allowing her to rub her scent along his skin. He dropped his forehead against hers, closing his eyes as the comfort from the animal flooded his body. She chuffed, and he chuckled at the impatient sound.

"Fine," he conceded and backed up.

He shifted, and his bear quickly changed his body, eager to meet its mate. The two animals butted heads, rubbing their sides together. He inclined his head towards the surrounding area, and Julissa ambled off at a leisurely pace. He followed suit, allowing his bear to take over entirely. The animal would keep them safe, of that he had no doubt.

JULISSA STRETCHED HER body as their bears gave them back control. She watched him as he shifted back. Rocco could feel her probes at their bond as she tried to figure out what was happening. His body was relaxed, and he was sure his face showed nothing, but she was privy to all that roiling emotion he hid beneath the surface. Their bond was tight; hiding from his mate would be a fool's errand. She stepped back while he inspected their room before he allowed her inside. It was close to two in the morning, but she ran the bath instead of showering.

Rocco smiled absently as she added the bath beads she'd found in the bathroom to the water. He made no moves to stop her. He could feel her determination to care for him, and after his nightmare, he would take the luxury his mate offered.

"Get in," she ordered him.

He snorted. "Sug, that tub ain't big enough."

"We'll fit." She assured him.

He chuckled softly but followed her orders. She let him get settled before she slid in on top of him. He grunted as she settled between his legs. His knees were high on either side of her, but for the most part, they fit. He closed her eyes as the hot water enveloped them. He luxuriated in the press of Julissa's heated skin, the touch more healing than sexual. Rocco kissed her shoulder.

"Tell me, my love." She prodded.

He sighed, knowing what she was asking. "My parent's mating was full of turmoil—fighting, jealousy, anger. I didn't want to even think about relationships for a long time, never mind mating.

She left him, and we moved from place to place for a while, running from him. When I was ten, he found and killed her during one of their fights."

"I'm so sorry, Rocco," she whispered, her voice thick with unshed tears.

He laid his cheek against the back of her neck, seeking comfort. Her bear filled her skin with power despite the animal being exhausted from their run.

He took a shuddering breath. "I don't want to fuck this up, Liss."

She grabbed his hand and kissed his fingertips, rubbing her cheek against his palm.

"There is no part of me that fears you, Rocco. Our mating would never be toxic so long as we communicate and set boundaries that we're both secure with." She paused... "Is that how you ended up at Winnie's house?"

"Not at first. There were so many other homes before then. I can't do chaos, so I would run at the first opportunity. I spent many nights on the streets of Eastfield before Silas found me."

"How old were you?"

"Twelve."

Two long years he'd been on the street. He

hated thinking about that time, but he'd long since dealt with the trauma from it. There were counselors that worked with the young shifters at Winnie's House, but Adina had personally taken him to therapy concerned with the anger that used to ride him. Julissa lowered her head.

"Don't sug," he ordered, butting against her shoulder. "I came out of it fine."

"The Knights adopted you?"

He chuckled. "Tried. It took me a while to settle into Winnie's house. But when I did, it felt safer there than risking another situation like my parents. The place was clean. The other shifters there kept to themselves for the most part. There was never all the yelling and fighting I had encountered at the other places. Adina..." he sighed, "I don't know. She took one look at me, and it was like she refused to let me go. I just...replacing my mother with her felt like a betrayal. Silas and Mason would hang out at the house when their mother volunteered. Silas and I clicked immediately, and we all started hanging out." He shrugged. "The rest is history."

"But you've satisfied yourself on the outskirts of their family."

"I'm more comfortable there. Adina fought it at first, but eventually, she understood."

Julissa slid her cheek against his chest. "Will it set you off if I ask about your voice?"

He shook his head. "In one of his drunken states, my father lifted me by my neck with his claws. It punctured my vocal cords. It was before I got my bear, so the healing took forever. It was the last straw for my mother."

She turned as much as she could and traced the tattoos on his neck. He'd gotten them to cover the scars from his childhood. She kissed his neck softly.

"Ain't no space in this tub for all that, mama," he said huskily.

"Out then." She said.

She grabbed a towel and wrapped it around her body. She turned and did the same for him.

He lifted her chin, "Taking care of me, sug?"

"Always," she swore to him softly. "You're mine to protect now. No more outskirts, Rocco Jamison. I'm showing you off."

He chuckled, lifting her. She wrapped her legs around his waist.

"Showing me off, huh?"

"That's fucking right." She declared, kissing him.

Thirteen

Before the sun sent its rays across the sky, Rocco's bear was waking him. Heat poured from Julissa, her body hot to the touch as she nuzzled closer to him. He cursed and rolled over quickly, his heart pounding. Panic confused him momentarily, and he could only stare down at his mate. Heat. He should've been ready for it; it wasn't like he hadn't been warned about what happened when sows mated. But he wasn't prepared for his own savage response. The enticing scent and warmth emanating from her body called to him, beckoning his bear. He needed...

He needed space first.

Fresh air to clear his mind before he did what his body was begging for. He quickly dressed, scrawled a hasty note, and vacated their cabin, taking his first easy breath once he reached a safe distance. Rocco stared back at the room and debated his next move. Julissa had one more meeting before they could leave town. Their next trip was a four-hour drive to the next sanctuary town. No way would either of them make it. They would be stuck here, so his first phone call should be to Silas to give him the schedule change. Except, it wasn't Silas' number he dialed.

Dallas answered on the second ring. "What's wrong?"

"PD," he said desperately.

"Talk to me, Rocco."

"Mating heat."

Dallas laughed. "I reminded you about this the other day. You good?"

"I don't know, PD."

"I don't know shit about bears except what I've learned from you. But we already talked with that elder bear. Everything will be fine." Dallas assured him with a chuckle.

"What if I hurt her, Pop?"

All his childhood memories threatened to rear up and drown him. The fights between his parents —the jealousy-led drinking binges that resulted in him and his mother being knocked around. All of it would take him under. He wasn't good enough for Julissa, despite her faith in him.

"She's yours, Rocco." The amusement left Dallas' voice. "That means she was built for you."

He nodded though Dallas couldn't see him.

"You are nothing like your sperm donor," Dallas continued.

Rocco heard him, but he looked in the mirror and saw his father's face daily. Dallas seemed to sense what he was thinking.

"Just think… which of my boys looks exactly like me, and which one acts just like me."

He had to chuckle because Mason was Dallas through and through, but Silas was his twin. That…strangely made him feel worlds better.

"Thank you, PD."

"Anytime, son. You need anything else from me?"

"No. I can handle it."

"Good. Then let me tell DiDi we may get more grandkids sooner than she thought."

Rock let out a rough laugh, his chest constricting with both longing and fear. The thought of a family of his own was as daunting as it was exciting.

"Good luck," Dallas told him before ending the call.

He took a deep breath and made his next call.

"The fuck, Rock?" Silas asked, his voice distracted.

"Need Keisha to push the next few meetings back a couple of days. Three at the most."

"Man," his best friend complained.

Rock heard him move around before his voice was clearer.

"What now?"

"Liss is going into heat."

Silas laughed. "Fuck. I forgot bears are different. You straight?"

He wanted to fuck his mate clear into the mattress, but he didn't tell his best friend that. He just grunted, to which Silas chuckled again.

"You need extra guards since you'll be down a few days."

He sighed and rubbed the back of his neck. That would probably be a good idea. "Yeah."

"I'll get Julian on it. Bears go into heat to make it easier for them to get pregnant, right? Her brothers finna be on your ass. That's good. We ain't been in a good fight in a while."

He laughed, his hands shaking as he wiped his face. "The fuck is wrong with you?"

"Just saying. You know how bears get down about their females."

Shit, he knew firsthand. He was already ready to die behind that woman. "You got me?"

"Always, Rock. Handle your business, and I'll take care of the rest. Congratulations, man."

"Thank you," he ended the call and went to get the things he would need to get him and his mate through the next few days.

He was glad that he had called both PD and Silas. They'd managed to calm the panic that had been taking him over. Now he could at least think clearly. He needed to talk to the guards on duty with him to give them a heads-up, and then he would take care of his mate. However, he would have to stay away from her for the duration of the meeting because he didn't think they'd get anything done if they were within touching distance. Even now, his bear thrashed against him, begging for release.

It would be a long morning.

JULISSA WAS CALLING Rock every curse word she could think of as she wrapped her meeting with the town alpha. She'd woken up alone and yearning for her mate, and he'd been nowhere to be found. If she'd followed her bear's instincts, she would've used his scent and hunted him down, but the note he'd left bedside had cautioned her against the action. God, mating heat. It wasn't as though Julissa hadn't extensively talked with her mother about it. Even with those conversations, nothing could have prepared her for the searing urgency that overtook her body.

Rocco had warned her last night. He'd rightfully asked her to put it off at least until they'd completed the meetings, and now she understood why. She wanted to rail and curse, but there was no time for that. Not when the urge to fight and then fuck with her mate was riding her hard. Byron had taken one inhale and told her that he couldn't drive with her today. He'd sent Harold, a cougar shifter who wouldn't be affected by her heat. Luckily for her, the alpha of their town was a wolf, so he didn't have an issue with it, though he'd been visibly uncomfortable.

She was shocked that she'd been able to get through the meeting. Julissa had gone over the points she and Silas had discussed, her leg bouncing the entire time. She was flushed and irritable as she got into the back seat of the SUV they'd rented. Rock had made himself scarce the whole meeting, which pissed her off. Maybe if he had been in the room, she could've concentrated a little bit more. Luckily for her, she'd attended many of her law school classes on scant hours of sleep, partially hung over, so she hadn't missed anything important during the meeting. Still...

It was nearing midafternoon when Julissa reached their cabin, and she was starving in more ways than one. She growled when she entered the room, and it was empty. Where in the hell was he? She stripped out of her clothes, unable to take the cloth against her skin. She was down to her panties and bra when she heard the door beep. She swung around when it opened, and her body went up in flames. Rock entered the room in all black, and she realized that had he been at that meeting, it wouldn't have happened.

She would've fucked him right in the middle of the whole city council. She growled, her bear riled at the sight of him. He came in with a bag of food, his hands up.

"Food first, sug, then I'll take care of all that heat," he promised softly, moving slowly.

Her eyes tracked him like prey across the room to her. She was afraid to move. Afraid she would attack him if he got too close. He must have sensed it because he hastily dropped her food on the table. The scent of the salmon rose, and her stomach growled. He set out their food, and still, she stood there, rooted to the spot, her body overheated and overwrought. He finally finished and walked over to her. She shuddered the moment his hand grazed down her shoulders.

"Easy, mama," he whispered.

Her body shook in need, her womb clenching, and her clit throbbing as the heat exploded with his nearness. He made a choked sound before his claws dropped. She could smell the wildness of his bear as it fought him. He scraped his teeth down her neck.

"You left me," she managed to choke out.

"I had to, Liss. The heat had my mind gone," he whispered against her skin.

"Need you," she whispered.

"Food, then fuck."

"Fuck. Now," she hissed.

His body shuddered. "Baby, if we start, you won't eat until tomorrow, on my life." He swore.

A tear slid down her cheek as her pussy contracted. He hummed and pulled her into his body. Her bear filled her, reaching for him, their magic intertwining. She would explode if he didn't touch her now. Instead of pleading with the man, she bypassed him entirely, her power rubbing against the bear inside him, roiling to the surface, turning his eyes darker. His pupils lit, and she smiled. Yeah, that was how she would get what she wanted.

Fourteen

Her heated skin scorched him. His baby was hurting, and Rocco could barely think straight. He woke this morning, his dick hard and his mind on nothing but fucking her until neither of them could walk straight. What must she be going through? He left their bed to give his bear release. It hadn't worked. And now his mate was using the animal to get what she wanted. That turned him on even more. He would never have to worry about running over this woman. Her bear called to him, broadcasting its wants across their bond.

Rocco's knees damn near went weak in need. Dallas had reminded him that they'd had the mating talk when he was a teenager, but nothing could have prepared him for the fire raging through his body. Rock had extended their stay another three days and gathered supplies for him and Julissa. He made sure that they remained separated while she got her work done, but they both paid for the distance. Now, his mate was in front of him halfway to naked, burning up, and his dick was hard enough to split through his pants.

Food, he reminded himself.

He could take the edge off for her and then feed her. After that, it was up. He slid his hand up her thigh, edging higher until he reached her sopping-wet panties. He begged his bear for control enough to pull back his claws. She whimpered.

"Easy, sug. I'll take care of you," he rumbled.

Rocco sighed in relief when his claws retracted. He inserted his fingers into her throbbing pussy and cursed as she squeezed down on him.

"Food," he whispered aloud this time.

He had to focus.

Fur rippled up and down his back as the bear pushed him for more. Julissa's claws pierced his shoulders as she rode his fingers. She threw her head back in ecstasy, and he bit the front of her neck. She screamed as she came, and he reluctantly pulled his fingers from her. He licked them clean, pulling her head down and kissing her. She sucked on his tongue, moaning. His body clenched as her anguished need transmitted across their bond. It took everything in him to pull away.

"Food, mama." He managed to say as he stepped back.

Her eyes were feverish, her bear watching him as he washed his hands. He pointed to the chair at the small table with shaking hands, unable to organize his thoughts, let alone speak. She sat obediently, which…lord, he just had to let her eat. He had to.

Otherwise…

Julissa devoured the food before her, her eyes never leaving his. Rocco got everything on the list for a sow in heat—salmon, lentils, sweet potatoes, high-energy foods, and fruit. The diner waitress had given him a smile and thumbs up when he'd ordered the disjointed foods. He was sure that bears weren't the only shifters that went into heat.

Once they were done eating, he skirted around her to the bathroom. Her eyes followed him, and he shivered in anticipation. Rocco started the shower in an attempt to wash off. She was a flame at his back as he stripped. He'd barely gotten into the shower stall before she was on him.

"Food, then fuck," she whispered, going down on her knees.

He cursed when she swallowed him down. He touched the back of her throat, and Rock saw stars. His eyes rolled back, and his body trembled. Between her hand tugging on him and the wet suction of her mouth, he wouldn't make it long. Rocco watched as his dick disappeared between her full lips. She was taking his soul and wasn't shit he could do about it. He pulled her up and pushed her against the wall. He entered her in one stroke, swallowing her gasp as he fought through her clenching pussy.

Fuck, he wouldn't make it.

It didn't stop him from driving into her, fucking her desperately. If it was just the physical, he could maybe gentle his strokes, but the emotion down their bond had his chest tight and his animal feral. Her claws scraped his back, and from the scent of blood, those marks would be deep and brand him for weeks. His bear growled in satisfaction. Rocco lasted longer than he thought, the water going cold around them as he pounded into his mate. She moaned loud and long as she came, pulling him behind her. Fire raced down his spine as he erupted inside of her. She kissed him, her body still undulating.

He turned off the water and guided them out of the stall, but they never made it past the bathroom sink. His dick hadn't softened. His bear wasn't done with her, and the heat hadn't yet released Julissa. The hot clasp of her pussy was addictive. He slowed his frenzied strokes, savoring every pull of her tight inner muscles. She growled in complaint, and he hissed as she bit down on his shoulder.

He chuckled. "Mean ass."

Rocco shoved in deeper, biting her back. Julissa screamed and tensed, another orgasm crashing over her. He was glad he had moved their departure because there was no way they would get any sleep tonight.

Fifteen

"I'm taking you out," Julissa announced.

Rocco looked up from his emails and squinted at his mate. They'd barely been back in their room for half an hour. They were in town number eight and had just wrapped their last meeting with the town alpha. So far, they had been getting next to no pushback from the towns, so he was starting to relax his guard just a bit. But complacent enough to go out on a date? He wasn't entirely sold on that.

He got a good look at Julissa as she moved closer to him. She wore a pair of leather pants painted on her curves and a Beyoncé concert tee underneath the camel trench she loved. High-top J's completed the outfit, and he smiled. He'd never seen her dressed down to go out. She had a million and one 'lounging' outfits, as she called them, but she never left their room less than done up. Her makeup was still immaculate, but a knit cap covered her long hair. She looked cute…approachable.

"Where are we going?"

"To a drive-in movie," was her answer as she shifted her stuff from her purse to a pouch around her waist.

He frowned and looked out the window. "It's the middle of the day, Liss."

"Do you want to change, or are you going to wear that?" She ignored his statement.

He looked down at the suit he'd worn to their meeting and back up at her. "I'll change."

The smile she graced him with warmed his heart. He dressed to match her fly—a pair of black jeans, Jordans, and his Tupac hoodie. He tucked his heat and texted Byron and Harold that they were leaving the room awhile. A drive-in movie during the day seemed silly, but his mate was taking him out. He would just see what the day brought. They loaded into the rented SUV, and he smiled at the bag full of snacks that Julissa pushed into the back seat.

Julissa loaded the address into the GPS, and they hit the road. He didn't mind the distraction.

They had wrapped their meeting early and would head to the next town in the morning. Their itinerary kept them on a tight timeline, but he was happy for these little pockets of rest. He thought Julissa going into heat would push them back in their schedule, but it had passed quickly. The fact that it had ended with her not being pregnant was a relief. He'd been a little disappointed, but he wanted more time with the two of them.

According to the GPS, they were thirty minutes from their destination. Julissa kept up her usual chatter next to him. He assumed that his bear would tire of the noise, but the animal loved the cadence of her voice and that soft tone she used when thinking aloud. He didn't think she really needed anyone to answer her musings. He was charmed by what he learned about her on the trip.

He pulled up to the theater and bought their tickets. He smiled as he realized it wasn't only a movie but also a car show. There were vintage cars scattered across the grass lot. He turned to her, and a smile took over her whole face.

"Surprise!"

He was touched. Excited. How in the world had she known this was happening? But then, he shouldn't be surprised. Julissa talked to everyone. The woman could find something to discuss with anyone she encountered everywhere they went. From a security standpoint, it had been frustrating, to say the least. But she enjoyed being around people, so he sucked it up. He tapped the steering wheel, momentarily worried that he should've brought back up. His eyes roamed the grass lot filled with shifters and cars, glancing at his mate. Seeing her happy expression, he wouldn't ruin her moment with practicality.

"Get out, Rocco. We'll be safe here. As you can see, it's mostly shifters." She read his mind. "According to the waitress in the restaurant where we had breakfast this morning, they meet once a month."

He didn't bother asking when she'd had time to find all that out from their short breakfast run. She amazed him. He grabbed his gun from the glove compartment and put it in his holster. He walked around and helped her from the car. She gripped his hand immediately, tugging him towards the crowd. Though he'd probably not admit it aloud, he was excited. He loved vintage cars, and the fact that Julissa had pulled that from him and gone out of her way to find this event warmed his heart.

She made him fall in love with her every day. He had expected a wave of love to overcome them the moment they bonded, but it was the little interactions that had sank him. He understood why she was so popular with the Motsi. Julissa paid attention to people and remembered details that most overlooked. He didn't talk much—he could admit that—but his mate treasured every word he spoke and noted the important things he'd slipped in their casual conversation. It was hard not to be charmed by that.

He lifted her hand and kissed her wrist. "Lead the way, sug."

Her smile both made his dick hard, and his bear settled. She was an amazing woman, and he was happy he'd put aside his insecurities and mated with her. Julissa led him around the grass lot, and Rocco relaxed so he could enjoy the time with his mate.

About an hour into their outing, his bear tensed within him. Rocco looked around, his chest rumbling as he spotted the male he'd seen in more than one of the towns they'd visited. Rock had spotted him three other times since the first town. He didn't believe in coincidences. He gripped Julissa's hand and pulled her away. Cars were parallel to each other in two lines, with food stalls and other vendors circling the show. Rocco tugged her closer to the stalls, away from the middle of the crowd gathering around the cars.

"I need you to stay put for a moment, love."

She furrowed her brows. "What's wrong?"

He cupped her chin. "Don't move from this spot, hear?"

She swallowed and nodded, her eyes darkening in lust at his tone. He kissed her, unable to help himself. He stepped away a moment later, scanning the crowd until he spotted the man. He circled the stalls, his bear protesting as they left Julissa unprotected. Predictably, the male sped his steps to get to Julissa. Rocco kept her in his peripheral as he came up behind the man. He growled as he pulled in the scent of the human. He pulled his heat and pressed it into the back of the man's head. The human's hands came up immediately.

"Talk to me," Rock said, his tone low and deadly.

"I...I work for the National Gazette." He hastily explained.

Rocco grunted.

"I wanted to ask Ms. Crespo a few questions about Mr. Knight's plans regarding Suncoast Energy's push to disband sanctuary cities."

"And it didn't occur to you to contact his office like the press is supposed to?" Rock released the safety.

His hands went higher, his body trembling. "I'm sorry. I know the protocol. I just thought..."

"You thought wrong," Rock informed him. "You've been following us."

He nodded. "Yes. Gathering information."

"Rocco," Julissa stepped closer to the male, and Rock growled. She sighed but paused her movement. "I can answer a few of his questions, and then we can get back to our day. Once his questions are answered, I imagine Mr...."

"Latimore."

"Mr. Latimore won't need to follow us anymore, right?"

Latimore nodded quickly, inhaling sharply when Rocco pressed his gun harder into his head.

"I swear."

Rocco clicked on the safety and stepped around the human. He put Julissa firmly behind him. "Ask your questions and then go. You don't get another warning."

"Understood." Latimore released a shaky breath.

JULISSA FED ROCCO, another piece of cotton candy before taking a bit herself. She danced as the sugar melted on her tongue. It had taken a few hours, but her mate had finally relaxed. She thought for sure he would make them leave after the reporter, but he had allowed her to distract him. He'd walked the reporter to his car and watched him go; that had helped. That and she'd fed him every sweet snack she could find from the different vendors. Her mate was self-possessed and sometimes grumpy but a sucker for sweets. She used that knowledge to her advantage the whole afternoon.

He was relaxed, but it hadn't stopped his watchful eye from roaming the crowd. Nor had it stopped his growls when someone got overly close or familiar with her. She was happy that her surprise for him pleased him. It was fascinating to see him open up as he talked to the different car owners. Mind, he still kept his words to a minimum, but the owners showed him all the engine parts and details about their cars. She didn't understand any of it but had loved how intense Rocco got about it all. He'd even gotten information from a couple of people.

Dark was now falling, and the movie portion of the event was about to start. She walked her mate back to their rental and led them to the back instead of the front seat. Though she wore sneakers, her feet still felt the hours they had walked around, so she was happy to be sitting. She settled in her seat but looked up when she felt his eyes on her. Rocco leaned over her, his arm behind her headrest, the other sliding between her legs on the seat.

"Thank you, my love," he said softly, nuzzling against her cheek.

The dark quiet of the car pressed around them, enhancing the intimacy. The smell of his cologne surrounded her. He was addicting. Her stomach fluttered, emotion filling her at the love she saw in his expression. It flowed down their bond, and her bear rattled her chest with a purr-like sound. He chuckled, his eyes lighting with his animal. He dropped small, soft kisses to her lips.

"Did you have fun?" she asked in between.

"I did."

He nipped her chin, moving down her neck, pushing her shirt collar aside so he could lick across his mating mark. Julissa shuddered as need slammed into her.

"Rock," she whispered.

"Yes, mate?" He scraped his teeth up her neck before sucking on her skin.

She squirmed as her sex clenched, her clit throbbing.

Rocco growled. "I can smell that pretty pussy."

Julissa threw her head back and closed her eyes. The way he talked to her during sex had to be top five of her favorite things about her mate. She cursed the fact that she'd worn tight ass pants. Unless she wanted to be ass naked in this car where anyone could walk up, she would have to behave. Her bear released its own growl.

"There's a blanket in my go bag," she whispered.

"Say less, ma," he kissed her hard.

She tangled her tongue with his and gripped

his chin to keep him in place. God, she loved this man. He pulled back and reached into the trunk for her bag. It didn't take him long to pull out the blanket she carried. He spread it over her lap, and Julissa hurriedly unbuckled her pants, sliding them down.

His hand snaked under the blanket. He bit his lip the moment he brushed his finger over her sex. She was wet, and his eyes lit, a rumble vibrating his chest when he realized. He kissed her neck as his fingers parted her pussy.

"Playing in this pussy is my favorite thing to do," he told her.

"You talk to me so nasty," she whispered, grabbing his head and pulling him to her for a kiss.

He chuckled and backed up, pulling her over onto his lap. She looked around, wrapping the blanket around her waist.

"Anyone can see us," Julissa hissed.

"These windows dark as hell."

He pulled his dick from his pants, and Julissa shut up because she desperately wanted to feel him inside her.

"Uh-huh. I thought that would shut you up," he laughed, bringing her down onto his erection.

She moaned, wiggling her hips to work herself fully onto him. They both sighed in pleasure once she was seated, taking him all the way in.

"Such a perfect fit," he murmured, sliding his hands under her shirt. "Ride this shit, sug."

How could she not follow that order? She was careful to keep the truck from rocking as she slowly slid up and down on his shaft.

"Feels so good," she moaned.

He gripped her ass and scraped his teeth along her neck. "You and this good ass pussy."

Julissa threw her head back, basking in the sensations. Rocco lifted his hips, and she grunted as he pushed deeper inside. He reached between them and thumbed her clit, and she jerked at the fiery jolt of pleasure. She wrapped her arms around his shoulders, kissing her mate. Darkness pressed around them; even the sounds of the movie couldn't puncture their intimate cocoon.

"I love you, Rocco," she whispered against his lips.

"I love you, Liss," he told her before devouring her mouth.

She rode him slowly, dragging out their pleasure. Soon though, between his fingers on her clit and him whispering in her ear, an orgasm built, vibrating her body.

"Almost," she whimpered, working her hips faster.

"Let me have it, Liss," he ordered, pulling her down so that he filled her completely.

He pressed down on her clit, and she shattered, gasping as he flexed inside her. Rocco cursed, filling her. Their ragged breathing was loud, their chests moving together. Julissa snuggled into his chest, humming her satisfaction. She was sated, the hours they'd spent on their feet catching up with her. His chuckle sounded against her cheek.

"You finna sleep through this whole movie," he teased.

"Fuck that movie," she slurred.

She smiled as his laugh bounced off the walls of the SUV. God, she loved that sound and especially loved the happiness she could feel from him on their bond. He tightened his hold on her, rubbing his cheek against the top of her hair. She didn't know when she lost the knit cap she'd been wearing.

"As soon as we get home, I plan to pamper the

fuck out of you. You deserve it. I've been so proud of you this trip." He declared.

Julissa's heart thumped, and tears clogged her throat. She lifted her head. "Rocco."

"Come, let's go back to the hotel so you can rest." He carefully lifted her from him.

She cleaned up with the wipes she'd packed and crawled into the front seat. She couldn't help but stare at Rocco the whole way back. She'd never thought she would make a love match. Not many of the women in her position did. The matings and marriages were arranged, their family's interest the only thing that mattered. Finding Rocco, claiming him was a blessing that she was fully embracing.

Sixteen

JULISSA LOST TRACK OF their movements somewhere around town number twelve. They were finally in town number twenty, and she was having hallucinations of how her bed would feel once she finally reached home. She could feel the Egyptian cotton on her skin and the weight of her linen duvet. She smothered a yawn while waiting on Rocco as he shopped at the small jewelry store attached to their current airport.

Most of their traveling had been driving. It was faster and more efficient, not to mention cost-effective, to navigate between the towns. Most of them were concentrated in the Midwest, so that was easy enough. Though, the three- and four-hour rides between them weren't entirely comfortable. Despite how hard it had been, she was glad her mate had accompanied her.

He had expressed his concern about her after she'd gone through heat, worried she would be too overtaxed. Though she had been exhausted after it, it wasn't enough to stop her. She was both happy and disappointed that she hadn't gotten pregnant. She would be more than glad to have kids with Rocco, but she wasn't quite ready. She and her bear were incredibly smug and satisfied with their choice of mate and how Rocco cared for her. She loved being mated to him.

"Julissa?"

She winced, forgetting that she was on the phone with her mother. That happened so much when Rocco was around. Her eyes followed him everywhere, a bit obsessed with him if she were being honest. She turned and faced the rest of the airport to keep him out of her peripheral so she could concentrate.

"Sorry, I'm here, mama. Just tired. This is our last town."

"How do you feel now that you've survived your first heat?" Therese joked.

She snickered. "Happy. I don't think I understood how mating would feel." None of the books she'd read on the subject had even scratched the surface.

"I'm very happy for you. I'm sure that's partly why you're exhausted."

Julissa's cheeks heated. "I'm not talking about that with you."

Therese chuckled. "I'm meeting with Adina today to start planning your mating ceremony."

She swallowed her sigh because there was nothing she could do about that. "Fine."

"I'm glad you see things my way," her mother laughed.

"Are you finally going to tell me why I've been picking furniture for the past month?"

"Oh…yeah. We moved your stuff into Rocco's new penthouse. I like the neighborhood. Did you know he lived so close to us? I thought surely he would stay on the Southside, but—"

"Please tell me you're joking?" Julissa cut her mother off.

"I talked to Rocco, and he's fine with it. I assumed y'all had discussed it." Therese said.

She spun around and narrowed her eyes at her mate as he stood at the register. "When in the hell did y'all do all this? Did he say you could move me in?"

"We've talked a few times. I can't remember his exact words," her mother hedged.

"Mama."

"Have you seen the article about you? It ran in a few papers. Your father was worried." Therese changed the subject.

Julissa frowned. "What articles?" Her eyes scanned the airport until she found a newsstand.

She rushed over and snatched up a paper, seeing a picture of her during one of the town halls she'd held. The headline proclaimed that shifters were taking on a giant energy conglomerate to save sanctuary towns.

"Oh shit," she whispered. She needed to contact Silas.

"Your father will probably call you, but be extra careful, love. That's a lot of attention."

"Rocco has me." She said absently, skimming the article. She quickly paid the vendor.

"Ok, well, I'll leave you to it." Therese ended the call.

Julissa sucked her teeth and tucked her phone. Therese had properly distracted her, but best believe, they would be circling back over her mother's high-handedness. Of all the things she'd expected her mother to say, moving her into Rocco's place wasn't one of them. She walked back over to the jewelry store to wait on her mate.

"What's wrong?" Rocco asked, guiding her towards the airport exit and their waiting SUV as he left the store.

They had long ago loaded their luggage from the jet into the SUV. He'd wanted to visit the jewelry store before they left. She changed the subject, unsure she wanted to reveal that her mother had already moved her into his space.

"What did you get her?" She pointed to his small bag. She had noticed him buying the little charms a few towns ago.

He smiled and pulled out the small box. She opened it and laughed at the jeweled armadillo. Julissa wondered if his niece would see the humor in it. Rocco revealed little parts of himself the longer they were on this trip. She enjoyed getting to know him. She passed him the paper she bought.

"Word's out."

He frowned as he glanced at the article. He hummed after a moment. "Silas will take care of it."

"Our mothers are planning the mating ceremony already," she informed him to change the subject. There was nothing they could do about the article until they reached town.

He grunted.

"I would ask if you want it small or large, but my mother won't care what either of us wants."

"Mama Di will reel her in. She knows me," he said confidently.

She shrugged because he'd never seen Therese in full planning mode, though she was sure if anyone could rein her in, it may well be Adina Knight. Before they got into the truck, Rocco reached in the back and grabbed a small tote that he called her 'go' bag. He'd been making her carry it when they got a little trouble around town number…six…no ten. It held necessities and a change of clothes, just in case. She didn't want to find out what the just in case was, but nevertheless, she kept the tote on her with the emergency stash.

Loading them into the truck, they were off to their last town. Julissa took a deep, cleansing breath and focused—just one more town to go.

ROCK STRETCHED HIS NECK and took deep breaths to calm his fidgeting bear. The animal was on edge, and he well understood. It had been at least a week since he'd shifted. That was long for him. Plus, he could feel Julissa's exhaustion. She had been great throughout the whole trip. She'd treated each town with the same respect and diligence, though he could tell they were all running together for her. From the first town to now their last, she'd worked hard.

He couldn't wait to get her back to his den.

He had every intention of pampering her the moment they arrived. While he'd never planned to be mated, he most enjoyed being able to spoil his mate. He thought about his friend's words. He hadn't expected the match that fate had picked out for him. Like Silas, he hadn't seen himself with someone like Julissa. At most, he envisioned someone that could relate to his life, but the difference between them seemed to fill in areas of his soul that had long been missing. Fate had chosen well for him. He felt her eyes on him.

"What?"

"My mother had my stuff moved to your apartment."

He grunted, unconcerned about that. His gaze returned to the back window and the car still following them. He'd thought they would've lost them once they left the main highway.

"She said you agreed. You don't think that's something we should've discussed."

"You told me to talk to your mother." He reminded her.

She waved her hands. "About the weather, about yourself. Not to tell her where to put my stuff at your new penthouse."

He grunted again. It was all the same to him. Therese chattered the same way her daughter did. But, unlike with Julissa, he'd tuned out a good portion of her mother's conversation. Had they talked about moving his mate? Probably. He vaguely remembered telling her that Mama Di was redoing his penthouse. Once Therese had gotten the okay from him to call him whenever she had not been shy about it. She'd called him about the apartment, yes, but sometimes the woman called just to talk to him. It was…odd. For the longest time, Adina was the only person outside of his friends to call and check-in. Now Therese.

"Adina is redecorating my place. I told your mother that she could offer suggestions that would be to your liking." He murmured, distracted.

Her eyes narrowed. "You didn't tell her to move my stuff?"

Rocco shrugged because…maybe. The woman talked a lot. Plus, she liked to sandwich apartment talk with other mundane subjects to catch him off guard. He'd been noticed it, but he let her rock because he didn't mind it.

Julissa sucked her teeth.

"Faster," he ordered Byron.

The bear had been their driver for the majority of the trip. He looked up at Rocco through the rearview mirror. "I'd clocked them about ten minutes ago."

He nodded, happy her father had sent someone competent. He reached into his go bag and pulled his gun from there.

Julissa gasped. "What's wrong?"

"Be ready," He told her.

"For what?"

He didn't know yet, but he wanted her ready if they needed to run. Byron punched down on the gas, and the truck took off. The car behind them sped up, and Rock cursed. That was all the confirmation he needed that they were being followed.

"Call Silas," he ordered Julissa, handing her his phone.

"I can call from mine."

"From mine, love. And not the first contact. Dial Silas two." He ordered.

She nodded and, with shaking hands, did as he asked. He'd given her the code to his phone a couple of weeks ago. She put it on speaker, and Silas answered after the first ring.

"What do you need?"

Julissa sucked in a sharp breath and looked to him for the answer. He inclined his head, and she nodded.

"We're being followed and are still another hour away from Summerville." She told him.

Silas grunted, and they could hear him typing on the other end. "I'm tracking your phone. I anticipated trouble in Summerville once that article came out, so I sent Julian ahead. Will you be able to hold them off until he gets to you?"

"They're only following for now. I'll make it work." Rocco said.

"Summerville is where the energy company is trying to take over. It's why I saved it for last. The coverage got them desperate, it seems. Stay safe, and I'll work on my end."

Julissa tucked Rocco's phone back into his go bag. She screamed a moment later as the car behind them rammed them. He cursed and reached over her and downed the window. Knowing the drill, Julissa unbuckled her seatbelt and hit the floor as Rocco fired at the car approaching car. It hovered alongside them, swerving to avoid his shots.

Byron cursed, and the truck jerked when one of their bullets hit their tire. He fought to control the SUV and keep it from flipping. It didn't work, and Rock grabbed Julissa, tucking her tightly into him as the truck turned over. Her screams filled his head as the airbags inflated next to them, their animal's panic scenting the air as the truck slid across the icy pavement and into the ditch. Only the radio sounded in the freezing night as Rock took stock of their surroundings.

"Liss?"

She groaned in his arms, and he released her slowly until she landed on the door.

"I'm…I think I'm good." she finally answered.

He used his claw to cut through his seatbelt and grunted as he worked himself down. It took some maneuvering, but they finally got out of the turned-over vehicle and took stock. Byron limped to the back, working on getting their suitcases from the truck.

"What do you want to do?" Harold asked, reloading his guns.

"We need to move in case they come back," Rock muttered. "How far are we from Summerville?"

"On foot? At least a couple hours."

Rock cursed and turned to Julissa. She was dazed but standing upright, which was the most important part. He looked around, but they didn't have a choice. They would need to make it on foot. He walked up to Julissa and rubbed his hands down her arms to soothe her.

"We'll have to make it in our bear forms. Are

you okay with that?" He asked, nuzzling into her neck.

She gripped the back of his head. "I'll follow your lead."

His bear growled in approval and pride.

"We gotta move, Rock," Harold called from the front of the SUV.

He looked up and saw the headlights cutting through the dark night. "Let's go, sug."

They rushed to the truck, and he grabbed their go bags instead of the suitcases. The car that had run them off the road had circled back. Harold and Byron fired off shots, and the car returned the favor.

"Shift, Liss," Rock ordered.

They would have to navigate the unknown terrain in the dead of winter. Fuck.

Seventeen

Julissa's body was trembling as fear filled her. She'd heard his order but couldn't get her body to cooperate. They'd been shot at more than once. She knew that her job was dangerous. She got that, but to the point where they were being fired at, scary shit. At most, she'd assumed she'd get trolling and hate mail. She hadn't once expected physical violence, and now she understood the extra guards.

"Here, sug," Rock ordered, and she rushed forward on trembling legs. He gripped her chin. "Breathe, baby. I'll keep us safe; I just need you to shake off the panic." He promised.

They could've been killed. She didn't call that okay, but she didn't argue. Her bear reacted to the power in his voice, shifting quickly, tearing through the clothes she was wearing. Julissa froze when another set of headlights pierced the night, illuminating the side of the SUV. She yelped when she heard more gunshots. She didn't know how many bullets her guards had left, which unlocked a new fear. Rock shoved a tote at her. She grabbed it between her teeth and took off toward the woods.

Rock lumbered behind her, and they were off. She heard the shots behind them and flinched every time they hit the trees beside them, but she didn't stop running. Rock was behind her, his larger body nudging her forward. She vaguely heard Bryon and Harold still shooting back, but after a while, the gunshots stopped. The four of them didn't stop running, however. She was happy to know that all of them had escaped alive. So far, anyway. They still needed to find the town and survive these frozen woods.

She was exhausted, but Rock nudged her to keep going. In her bear form, Julissa was aware of everything in the forest. The sound of the animals scurrying away from them, scents of the wood's inhabitants, and even though she didn't feel the cold, the biting wind brushed through her fur.

Rocco navigated it all, expertly skirting lurking

campers, howling wolves and other animals. How he knew which direction they were going, she didn't know. Instinct bade her follow her mate. She trusted him implicitly to get them to safety. She didn't know how long they ran, but soon, she could smell the scents of a nearby town.

Her mate stopped her and shifted. Julissa did the same, damn near falling out of her animal form. She shuddered as cold air assaulted her body. The tote fell at her feet, and she hurriedly dove into it, pulling out the hoodie and yoga pants that Rocco had made her pack. She'd thought he was being overly cautious, but she thanked his foresight. The thick socks would have to do since she hadn't packed shoes in the bag. She would never make that mistake again. She looked at Rocco and gasped at the blood on his side.

"You were hit," she whispered, rushing to him.

He pulled her into his chest. "I'm fine, sug, just a graze."

The phone he packed in his bag was buzzing. He pulled it out, typed furiously, and tucked it back in the bag. He winced as he bent down to put on his pants. Julissa hurriedly helped him into his shirt.

"Come. Julian was able to clear the town," he told them softly. "Byron, you and Harold in front; I'll take the rear."

She gripped his hand tightly as they left the woods and moved through the town. There were police everywhere. Rocco marched her through the confusion, ignoring the local cops and heading straight for a small motel. He knocked on a room, and it opened. Julian Chase cursed as he saw them, grabbing Rock into a hug. Rocco grunted in pain.

"Fuck," Julian spotted the blood. "I got worried when I saw the state of your car. Hurry in."

He pulled them into the room. There were more than five shifters, stern looks, in all black, armed to the teeth. The only one she recognized was Julian, which was only because she'd seen him at a distance at Motsi functions. She looked around and took a deep breath. Julissa knew she needed to call her father, but that would have to wait until she could get her feet beneath her. All the adrenaline she'd been operating on was quickly leaving her body and leaving her a trembling mess.

"You okay, Julissa?" Julian eyed her.

She nodded, unable to speak.

"Rock, call Mama Di. She losing her shit."

Rocco was watching her, his eyes taking in all the things she thought she was successfully hiding.

"Room, first. Let me settle my mate," he rumbled.

"I got you two a room right next door. I'm staying until the meetings are done," Julian informed them, walking them to their room.

Julissa had never been so happy in her life to see a motel bed. She stood in the middle of the carpet until Julian left the room. The moment he did, her legs weakened. Rocco caught her before she hit the floor.

"Shower, then sleep, baby," he murmured, lifting her into his arms.

She nuzzled into his neck, her bear reaching out for his. His power surrounded her until she was warmed from the inside. Tears ran down her face as her brain finally processed how close they'd been to being killed. Julissa had lived a sheltered life, and this night had emphasized that better than anything could have. She owed her father and brothers apologies for all that they'd kept her safe from. Rocco said nothing, just holding her tightly as she cried. He put her on the bathroom vanity and held her while she broke down.

Julissa shuddered as she gathered her tattered nerves together. She gripped her mate tightly, not yet ready to separate from him. Her bear rumbled her chest in contentment.

"Better?"

She nodded in answer. His growly voice settled her like nothing ever had. Lifting her chin, Rocco studied her face before nodding himself. He pulled back and started the shower. She didn't move until the steam filled the place, watching him as he undressed. She was next, his hands gentle as he stripped her. There was no sexual heat, just the comfort of her mate taking care of her. She traced the puckering skin where his wound was healing with trembling hands.

She broke their tense silence reluctantly. "We still have to make those meetings."

He stiffened. Though she'd only known Rocco for a couple of months, she knew he was protective of her. She could well imagine what his instincts were telling him to do. Though he disguised the anxiety on his face, she could feel it along their bond. He had a superb poker face, but Rocco was losing his shit. Julissa didn't want to push him, but she had a job to do. He stared at her for long moments, not saying anything. She lifted her chin and met his gaze.

"No town hall, just the meeting with their alpha," he demanded.

She nodded. She could make that work. She'd call Silas and review the talking points again, but she would finish this job come hell or high water.

"Come on, sug." He lifted her and stepped them into the shower. "When we get home, you'll be able to soak and forget this day happened."

That sounded like heaven.

The first blast of hot water succeeded in relaxing her the rest of the way, and sleep seemed to slam over her. Staying awake was no longer an option.

ROCK STARED DOWN AT his sleeping mate, and his heart rate finally slowed. He'd been in situations much more dangerous than the one they'd been in tonight, but nothing had scared him more. He thanked every deity looking out for him that the men sent after them were amateurs. The men had easily given up once they'd entered the woods;

a professional would've kept chase. It was probably the only thing that had saved them. They'd been outnumbered and certainly out-gunned. Keeping Julissa safe had been his number one priority, and the weight of that had had fear coursing through his body the entire trip through the woods.

Being on the street for two years had prepared him to survive anywhere, but he had worried that his mate wouldn't make the trek through the forest. The two-hour impromptu hike would've been difficult for anyone. Pride filled his chest because she had navigated the miles between them and the city without falling behind. Her bear had easily submitted to his, and the animal inside of him rumbled his chest in deep satisfaction.

Rock sighed and pulled out his phone. Now that his mate was settled, he needed to settle the rest of his family. He dialed PD first, knowing Adina was hovering. The call didn't even ring before it disconnected, and a video chat call came through. He shook his head, knowing Adina would want eyes on him.

"Oh, Thank God," Adina answered her husband's phone. Her gaze raked his body as much as it could.

He made sure to keep the phone tilted up. The wound on his side was still healing. In an hour, it would be gone, but he didn't put it past Adina to notice.

"I'm good, Mama." He said immediately, his bear riled by her anxiety.

Adina started crying, though she never took her eyes off him. "Why is the phone so close?"

He cursed because nothing got past that woman, whether she was distraught or not. "Ma."

"The boy said he fine, DiDi. Cut that out," Dallas fussed, taking the phone from his mate. "Both of you are fine?"

"Yeah. We ran into some shit, but we expected them to put up a fight around Summerfield. Julian's here now, so I have backup."

"When are you coming home?" Dallas asked.

He looked at Julissa and sighed again. She'd been insistent that they carry out the meetings as scheduled. He admired the fight in her, but God, Rocco wanted her somewhere safe. He gripped the back of his neck and closed his eyes.

"After the meeting with the town alpha."

Dallas grunted. "I understand."

"Please keep yourself safe," Adina ordered.

A slight tilt of his lip and grunt was his answer.

"I love you, Rocco," Adina told him.

"You too. I'll let you guys know when we head out," he promised before ending the call.

He braced himself for the next call he had to make. He already had the number in his phone. Rocco had talked to the bear before. He'd had to in order to do the work he and Deena did with the women's shelter. Part of keeping the women safe counted on the tri-council stepping in once informed about the abuse. He'd never had any issues with Councilman Crespo doing what he could to help the shifters he ruled.

But this was a whole other set of circumstances. This was dealing with the man's only daughter —Rocco didn't know how he would react. The councilman answered quickly.

"Jamison." He growled.

"She's fine, sleeping off her adrenaline crash," Rock assured her father.

"What happened?" Micah asked, relief evident in his voice.

"We were ambushed outside of town. I'm sure Byron already reported to you."

Micah grunted. "And my daughter?"

"She's wrapping the last meeting in the morning, and we'll head home after. I'll have her call you when she wakes up."

"I…" Micah cleared his throat. "Byron told me you took care of her. I wasn't sold on your mating initially; maybe a part of me still isn't. But, thank you."

Rock gripped his phone and kept the slick comment on the tip of his tongue to himself. He wasn't a father yet but he could appreciate Micah's worry.

"She'll call you later." He ended the call, done with the conversation.

He understood he wasn't good enough for Julissa but didn't relish having her father lay it out for him. He knew they would have plans for their only daughter. He imagined it included a male who could bring more to their family, be it money or cache. The Motsi were meticulous about their matings and marriages. But Julissa was his now, and he would care for her much better than anyone Councilman Crespo could've chosen for her. Instead of crawling into bed with her, he slipped outside. Julian was in the outside hallway on the balcony overlooking the parking lot, a drink in his hand, his mind a million miles away.

"She settled?" Julian asked, passing Rock a glass.

"Just."

His friend sighed and poured Hennessy into the cup. "They shot your shit up. It fucked with my head for a few moments."

Rocco grunted. One thing about Julian, he'd never had issues expressing the way he cared for those in his circle. Rock envied him that.

"It takes a lot more than that to take me out." He reassured him.

Julian studied him before smiling. "How is it?"

Rock didn't have to ask him what he meant. Of all of them, Rock had been the last person to even consider mating. He hadn't seen it in the cards for himself.

"She's amazing."

"I already knew that. I want to know how your bear is handling it." Julian smirked.

"I..." He shook his head and sipped. "I thought it would be uncomfortable, but she has this way of soothing the animal."

"Nightmares, all that?"

He shrugged. He couldn't say they'd gone away,

but having Julissa in bed with him had certainly curbed them.

"Tell me about the meeting tomorrow." Julian prodded.

"Silas canceled the town hall meeting. I don't want to risk her in a large crowd, so we just have the meeting with the Alpha in the morning."

"I'll have your back regardless."

Rocco nodded, knowing that whole-heartedly. They had all been friends for years, and he'd learned he could count on their word.

"Go tend to your mate. I'll see you in the morning." Julian told him.

He knocked back the rest of the liquor in his glass, wincing at the taste. Though he hadn't spared a prayer in years, he sent one up that his mate would come out of all this safely.

Eighteen

If Rocco had to sum up the trip, he would call it successful. They'd only been attacked once, and he'd safely brought his mate home. That had been his ultimate goal. Whether or not Julissa had succeeded at her job, time would tell. He'd seen firsthand the many months it would take for any of Silas's work to pay off.

He looked down at his sleeping mate, tucked into his side. He carefully unbuckled his seat to give her just a moment more rest. Unlike him, she wasn't used to the heavy schedule. Now that they were home, all the details regarding merging their life were pushed front and center. First thing, though, she would be going home with him. That wasn't a debate. He wanted Julissa's scent in his den.

His new den.

Would she like the place? It had been years since he'd last been in the penthouse. The last time had been to install the new tub in the primary bedroom. The same bathtub he promised his mate a soak in. Just yesterday, before the attack, she was fussing about her mother moving her in without asking. Would that still be the case? He kissed the top of her head.

"Up, mama," he murmured.

It took her a moment, but she finally sighed and sat up. "Home?"

"Mmhmm."

She stretched. "I want the bath you promised me."

He gripped her chin and kissed her. "Tonight?"

"Mmhmm," she hummed. "Hot, hot."

"Done. You hungry?"

"Not just yet." She snuggled closer to him, swinging her leg over his.

He refused to laugh at this silly woman. He loved how affectionate she was. As a whole, shifters were tactile creatures, and Julissa was no exception. Touch seemed to be his mate's main love language. Were it not for the Knights, he didn't know that he would've been ready for it.

"We should probably grab something on the way. I don't know if Mama Di stocked the new fridge."

She slid her hand beneath his sweater, her warm palm resting against his heart.

"My mom did it. So at the very least, we should be able to find something for you to cook me."

He laughed. "Food delivery it is."

She smiled up at him, her eyes sparkling.

Julian stopped at their seat, breaking up their cocoon. "You got it from here, Rock?"

"Yep." He dapped his friend. "I appreciate you."

"You know how we do. Good night, Julissa."

She straightened in her seat and fixed her face into one she used for work. "Thank you, Julian."

Jules nodded and raised his brows, smiling. Rocco knew he would hear shit from his friends about his proper mate.

"Let's go, sug." He ordered.

They descended the jet, and his car was exactly where Silas said he'd dropped it off. He dismissed Byron, knowing her father had probably ordered him to follow them home. Rocco had his mate for now and would work out with Micah about her security later. He loaded his trunk and helped Julissa into the car.

They were silent on the drive to his place, which put Rocco on edge. Julissa was never quiet. In the weeks they'd traveled, he could count on one hand the number of times his mate had kept her thoughts to herself. She expressed even the small ones that most would keep to themselves.

He tapped his fingers against the steering wheel as he parked, debating his next words. Before he could offer to take her home, Julissa leaned over and kissed his cheek.

"I can feel your bear's agitation. There is nothing wrong. I am just drained. Tomorrow I'm sending Silas all my notes and spending the rest of the weekend in pajamas."

He released the breath he'd been holding. That sounded perfect to him. He helped her out of the car, and they walked around to his trunk.

She frowned. "I only need that bag." She pointed to the smallest one. "The rest can wait until tomorrow."

"I'll come back and get them." He told her, pulling out his bag as well.

"Tomorrow, love," she insisted, rubbing her cheek against his chest.

He didn't think he'd ever tire of her affections. He was tense the whole elevator ride to the fourth floor. He locked the elevator doors for his floor and guided her to the front door. Julissa paused a foot from the door and allowed him to enter first. His eyebrows winged high in surprise as he entered his apartment. The place was immaculate and tastefully decorated. Not that he doubted Adina; she had exquisite taste. The fact that the space was so…him. It was to his taste, and he didn't know how the two women had accomplished that. He could see where his mate had made her choices. It blended seamlessly into his.

He'd expected it to be full of leather, but the women had blended rich velvets in the furniture and curtains that covered the floor-to-ceiling windows. It was an open floor plan, so he could see from the door to the other end of the room, where a reading space was set up. Two full bookshelves lined the wall with a plush armchair that was probably for his mate. She read in her spare time; he knew she would love the space. He was anxious for her to see it. He inhaled and filtered through the scents finding no recent ones.

"It's safe, Liss." He called to her.

She came in and gasped. "Oh, this is beautiful!" She walked the length of the living room, her face excited. "I can't believe you were living downstairs when this was up here the whole time."

He grunted because there was nothing he could say to that. But he felt a lot more would change with her in his life. He couldn't wait.

He would give his mate an hour…hour and a half tops. No way would he spend the whole of his afternoon with her brothers staring him down across the table. Rocco adjusted the collar of his v-neck sweater and debated lowering his fangs. Liam and Lachlan had been on bullshit from minute one, and he was near his tolerance for it. Therese had invited him and Julissa out for a family dinner under the guise of them all getting to know each other. He had better things that he could be spending his Saturdays on, especially since he could still feel Julissa's exhaustion from the trip.

But she wanted to see her family; most importantly, he was cementing his place in his mate's life. The more people that saw them together, the fewer people he would have to knock over the head behind her. So, he was all for dinner at one of the most popular restaurants in Eastfield. Plus, though he would never admit it out loud, Liam's restaurant was one that he frequented. His chef was exceptional.

Liam growled again, adjusting in his seat across from Rock. Julissa sucked her teeth and hit her hand against the top of the table.

"What is your problem, Liam?" She snapped.

"I want to know how he plans to keep you safe when he's still doing street shit for Dallas Knight." Her brother crossed his arms over his chest.

"Liam," Therese chided.

But he continued. "Not to mention, his building is filled with females who are in dangerous situations. What's to stop one of their mates from attacking your building?"

His chuckle held no amusement. "I wish the fuck they would."

He didn't raise his voice or even get irritated. While her brother was being an asshole, he had a valid point. Rocco had security measures in place, but it wasn't something just anyone would know.

Julissa's mother turned a smile at him. She was sitting right next to Rocco, opposite her husband.

"Helping battered women is admirable." Therese soothed.

"Lord, mama, don't go bragging to your friends about it. It could bring undue attention to the building," Julissa reminded her.

Therese held her hands up. "I'm just saying."

Rocco warmed. His mate understood why he did what he did and supported him fully.

"My staff speaks highly of you." Micah looked impressed. "Do you just help bears?"

He shook his head. "Any shifter. I work with one of the women's shelters in the city. Despite how well run they are, it's no place for kids. I would rather they have someplace more stable."

Therese rubbed his shoulder. "I love that."

They were impressed by work that he would be doing no matter his circumstances. It just so happened that he was in a place to help the women.

"It's dangerous," Liam said stubbornly.

"That aside, will we have to worry about your hands in her trust fund?" Lachlan cut in.

"You're being ridiculous." Julissa snapped.

Rocco sat back in his chair and put his arm around Julissa's seat. He liked his mate sticking up for him. He rubbed the back of her neck, feeling her anger down their bond. His touch soothed her bear, and Julissa relaxed, though she still mugged her brothers.

Lachlan waved off his sister. "Stay out of this, Julissa. It's between males."

Julissa sat forward. "I wish I would just sit here while you disrespect my mate."

"We can go somewhere else and discuss this." Lachlan threatened.

"I ain't got shit to hide from my baby," Rocco said, not moving.

He gave her brother a taunting smile, to which Liam growled, his eyes flashing with his bear.

Micah growled from his seat. "Cut it out, both of you. You can see their bond from way over here." He grumbled. "Y'all already tried to scare the man off. Clearly, it didn't work."

"Thank you, Dad."

"It's beautiful," Therese said. "Rocco, are you still going to work for Silas?"

He turned his attention to her mother. "Until

it affects Liss, I'll probably keep protecting him. It keeps him out of trouble and me busy."

Micah chuckled.

"Well, no pregnancy this heat, but—"

"For God's sake, Therese, I don't want to hear about my daughter in heat." Micah cut in.

"I just wanted to ask about kids," she fussed.

Rocco couldn't help the small smile that lifted his lips. Thinking of Liss pregnant with his baby made him and his bear happy. For the longest time, he hadn't seen it for himself.

"As far as I am concerned, their kids will be hatched from eggs. I don't want to hear otherwise." Micah sliced his hand in the air to dead the conversation. "Where in the hell is dinner?" he asked, looking around.

"I'll go check," Liam left the private room they were in.

Rocco hid his smirk as Therese sucked her teeth.

"Fine."

"I didn't know you owned the garage over on 4th until the contract negotiations started. I've taken my car there a few times." Micah changed the subject.

"Oh yeah? What kind of car?" Rocco would much rather talk about cars if he had to pick.

If it went to the place off of 4th, it had to be a classic car. They only worked on vintage ones. It was the first garage he'd opened, and he'd only done it so he would have a place he trusted to take his own car.

"It's an Aston Martin DB5."

"No shit, the '64?" He was impressed.

Micah nodded. "I said I would do the work myself, but then I get caught up with other stuff. Did you restore the Lincoln yourself?"

"I did. That's usually what I'm doing on my downtime."

Micah sat forward, bracing his elbows on the table. Both Therese and Julissa groaned, so Rocco could only assume her father was like him in his love of cars.

Nineteen

The following day, Julissa rolled out of their new bed, groggy and searching for her mate. She was enjoying being back in town. She'd been looking forward to being in her own bed, but being in Rocco's was even better. She would probably still be asleep if she hadn't felt Rocco's absence. After dinner with her family last night, they'd spent the rest of the evening snuggled on the couch watching movies. Today was dinner with his family.

She wasn't worried about that too much. She'd never had any issues with the Knights, and they couldn't be anywhere near as bad as her brothers had been last night. She'd wanted to clock them both. The only thing that stopped her from getting violent was the fact that she could feel Rocco's mood the whole dinner. Not once was he anything other than content. She'd expected anger, aggravation even, but nothing had ruffled the man or his bear.

She left their bedroom. Julissa paused in the hallway, letting that sink in.

Their bedroom.

Because they had mated on the road, it hadn't quite felt real, but being in a shared space that was theirs...It brought everything into clarity. Rocco was hers. She smiled and carried on through the apartment, searching for him. She could hear the clinking sounds of weights, so she followed her ears to the home gym on the second level. He was stretched out across the bench press. Her body warmed, sleep a thing of the past. Seeing Rocco's big body laid out on the gym equipment unlocked a new fantasy she hadn't realized she had. She walked closer to him and waited.

Once he hung up the bar he was lifting, she straddled his lap. "Why are you up so early?" She whined.

He skimmed her thighs. "Habit, plus I need to get used to a new place."

She hummed and kissed his sweaty chest.

"Don't come in here starting shit," he grumbled,

sitting up and gripping her ass. His dick rose beneath her. "You hungry?"

"I could eat." She slid her hand into his basketball shorts, lightly brushing the head of his dick.

He chuckled. "You finna find yourself bent over this bench, lil mama. Behave."

"Yeah, I'm trying to sign up for that," she murmured, letting her claws out and sliding them down his stomach.

He hissed, his eyes glowing, his bear rumbling his chest.

"We have plenty of time before we need to head out." She said coyly.

"Fast ass," he growled, lifting his shirt off her.

He stood with her in his arms. She thought he was taking her to their room, but he didn't. He put her down and spun her around fast enough to take her breath away. He pushed down on the middle of her back until she was braced against the bench, ass in the air.

He kicked her legs wide and ripped the seat of her panties. He left the waist, using it to hold her in place as he slammed into her. Julissa could only curse as he made good on his word. She took every stroke, throwing her hips back, moaning his name.

"This what you wanted, right?" He husked out, slowing his strokes to a torturous speed.

"Yes!" Julissa screamed as he hit her spot.

Maybe she could've lasted, but his nails dug into her waist as his dick rubbed across that spot repeatedly. It didn't help that Rocco talked her through the orgasm, tightening her body. His rough voice, combined with the sounds and scent of their lovemaking, tipped her over the edge. She screamed as she came, squeezing and tightening the walls of her pussy, determined to have him right behind her.

"Take that shit, then," he growled, his strokes speeding erratically until he shoved into her one last time, climaxing.

Julissa chuckled, her legs weak as lethargy took over her body. This was a way better way to start the day.

HOURS LATER, JULISSA was still thinking about their morning session. The noise around her was soothing, though some would find it otherwise. But, the happy squeals of the children had her smiling as she sipped her wine. From the moment they entered the Knight's house, Julissa had felt welcomed. It was a much different reception than what her mate had gotten from her brothers.

"How was your trip?" Celine asked her. "Well, outside of the trouble you guys had?"

She smiled. She'd seen Celine at several Motsi events and had never seen her this personable and open. Mostly the woman kept to herself, so Julissa had never gotten a chance to get to know her. She found the woman sweet and funny.

"It was exhausting, but I really enjoyed it." She told her. "Having Rocco with me was a bonus."

Celine's eyes sparkled. "I bet. I'm so happy for Rocco. And you, of course," she hurriedly added.

Julissa laughed. "I understand what you mean."

"Are the two of you settling into the penthouse?" Adina asked, joining them at the table.

"You did an amazing job. It managed to blend both of our tastes." She gushed.

"I helped too!" Sariyah added, coming into the kitchen to swipe a biscuit.

"Excuse you, munchkin," Ms. Iris fussed.

Sariyah gave her an unrepentant smile and rushed from the room, her stolen food in hand. Julissa smiled. The little girl was beautiful and clearly enamored with her Uncle Rock. Her heart fluttered seeing Rocco in his element with his family. If she leaned over, she could see him outside bouncing his nephew around as he talked to his best friends. She thought his stoicism was with strangers, but he was just as quiet around the Knights, only sporadically adding to the conversation. Oddly, it was reassuring. He didn't put on airs, and was honest, no matter the situation. It added a sense of security to their mating. She would never have to worry about waking up one day and Rocco being a totally different person.

"Therese told me she was getting feedback from you," Adina said.

"She was sending me random text messages with pictures asking me to make choices. I thought I would come home to my apartment completely redecorated." She confided.

The women laughed. The conversation between them all flowed easily, and Julissa relaxed, feeling like she'd known these people for years. Soon though, Iris was done cooking.

"Julissa, can you go grab the boys and let them know it's time for dinner?" Ms. Iris asked.

She hopped from her stool and headed for the back sliding doors. They were sitting around the pool. She took a moment to admire them all. Every last one of them was fine, but something about the men, passing babies between the four of them, caught her breath. It was beautiful to witness. Rocco had a radar for her because his eyes met hers the moment she stepped outside. He waved her over.

"Dinner is ready," she told them as she reached Rocco sitting in the lounger.

He slid his hand up her leg, crooking his finger. She bent over, and he grabbed the back of her neck, bringing her closer for a kiss.

"You doing okay?" He asked her softly.

"I love your family," she assured him.

The smile he gave her was everything. Their whole relationship flashed through her mind. If she'd made any different decisions, they might not have met. What would her life look like without him in it? She didn't know, nor did she care to find out. She was riding with him forever.

From her dream job to the man currently staring at her as though she were the only person in his world, Julissa had more than she'd ever dreamed she would have.

Twenty

Epilogue

Rocco waved off the waiter in front of him, forgoing the champagne he offered. If he was getting through this night, he needed to be sober. Ultimately, his mate had been correct, her mother wanted a big to-do, and Therese got it. Their actual mating ceremony had been intimate, but the woman had not budged on the celebration. Five hundred or more shifters moved around the ballroom, the décor outdoing any magazine Rocco had ever seen. In another hour, there were supposed to be fireworks going off outside. He sighed and flexed his fingers, wishing for a blunt.

"You need this more than me," Silas said, holding out his hand.

Rocco gratefully took the vape. "How many people in this motherfucker?"

Silas snickered. "How you feel?"

"Good. That's my baby." He passed the vape back. "Have you given your team the news?"

He nodded. "They worked hard to get those votes. Now the challenging part starts, but getting an injunction on the energy company will give us more time to work."

"Do you think Julissa will be in any danger of blowback?"

Silas shook his head. "You know how it goes. They're pussies, and once their intimidation doesn't work, they move on to throwing money at it."

Rock grunted and hit the vape again. He met eyes with his mate across the room, and she smiled. His bear moved within him, settling at the happy look on her face. His gaze moved over the rest of the room, and he narrowed his eyes as he spotted Dallas chatting with some wolf shifters who had never attended Motsi events before. Their faces were businesslike, and it put up Rock's antenna.

"What's PD up to?" He asked his best friend.

Silas chuckled. "Best leave that for later. You have your mate now. Gotta put that Rock away."

"Never that," he murmured.

He couldn't just turn that part of him off. That beast was still lingering, waiting to come out when needed. For all the Knight family had done for him, he would go to war for them. He now added Julissa to that number. His eyebrows winged high when Julissa nodded her head towards the balcony. Heat moved through his body, his bear attuned to her every need. He gave her a subtle dip of his chin and turned to his friend. Silas cracked up.

"Gon' head, man."

He passed the vape back to Silas and headed for the balcony where he'd first met his mate. The air was damp, warming with the coming of spring. None of that touched him as he slid into the shadows, waiting. It took another five minutes before he sensed her, his body tensing in anticipation. Not unlike the first night they'd met. Those months ago, he hadn't felt good enough for her...not that it was any different now.

But, with the reassurance and love she poured into him, he was in a place of acceptance. Julissa would defend him against anyone, including him-self. His mate didn't play about him. Her heels clicked as she sauntered to him, her hips swaying the red sequined dress that was poured onto her curvy body.

God damned, that woman was bad a fuck.

And all his.

The smile she gifted him with when she finally came around the column where he was hidden made his dick hard. It was confident; none of the apprehension from that other night clouded her face. She was a woman who knew she had him wrapped around her fingers.

"I missed you," she whispered, stepping into his space.

Her scent rose between them, curling around his heart, riling his bear. But the man...the man was soothed by it. He leaned into the space be-tween her neck and shoulder, inhaling, his body relaxing despite wanting to bend her over the rail and sink into her.

"How much longer we gotta stay?"

She cupped the back of his head with one hand, using the other to slide across his waves. "Say the word, my love, and we can bounce."

"What's the word?"

She chuckled and whispered the nastiest thing he'd ever heard her say. His knees went weak. When he thought of how different his life would be had he allowed his self-doubt to win, he clutched her tight. He would still be in that lonely darkness on the outskirts of the life his friends had tried to build for him. They'd all wanted him immersed in their lives, thoroughly enjoying the family's success, but he'd been reluctant, indulging in the darkness that had been his life for so long. Instead of allowing it, Julissa had shone her light on him, dragging him from the edge. He would never take her for granted.

"I love you, Liss," he whispered, claiming her mouth before she could return the sentiment.

For her, he would be the man she believed him to be.

Also available from Dria Andersen

Chasing Savannah
Hers to Call
Destiny Series
A Destiny Awakened
Destiny Revealed
Escaping Destiny
Haven Series
Haven
Soulbonded
Hellbound
The Hamilton Brothers
The Friend Contract
The Alpha Accord
Georgia Arcana Series
Surrender to the Moonlight
Magic in the Moonlight
The Knight Series
To Her Rescue
For Her Safety
Short Stories

Porsha's Wolf
One Night One Bite

Author's Note

Firstly, let me say that content warnings abound for this story. There is mention of child abuse, domestic abuse, and drunken abuse. Though it doesn't happen on page, some of it is spelled out, though not graphically. Rocco has gone through some stuff and it has shaped him. That trauma may be a little rough for some to read, but I try not to be too explicit. As usual, there is a lot of cussing in this book, y'all know how I do. There are sex scenes, with explicit language, and there is violence. If I miss any, please feel free to let me know. I try to be very careful about it warning readers.

The story is novella length, so short and sweet. These two were fairly easy to write and I love when that happens. As usual, it's an easy and fun love and I hope you guys enjoy. Thank y'all for taking this ride to back to Eastfield with me!